THE WAGER OF A WALLFLOWER

REVENGE OF THE WALLFLOWERS
BOOK 3

LINDA RAE SANDE

The Wager of a Wallflower

V1

ISBN: 978-1-946271-76-1

Cover photograph © Period Images

Cover art by Mandy Koehler Designs

Edited by Katrina Teele-Fair

https://www.lindaraesande.com

The Enigma of a Widow

The Secrets of a Viscount

The Widowers of the Aristocracy

The Dream of a Duchess

The Vision of a Viscountess

The Conundrum of a Clerk

The Charity of a Viscount

The Cousins of the Aristocracy

The Promise of a Gentleman

The Pride of a Gentleman

The Holidays of the Aristocracy

The Christmas of a Countess

The Knot of a Knight

The Holiday of a Marquess

The Snow Angel of a Duke

The Heirs of the Aristocracy

The Angel of an Astronomer

The Puzzle of a Bastard

The Choice of a Cavalier

The Bargain of a Baroness

The Jewel of an Earl's Heir

The Vixen of a Viscount

The Honor of an Heir

The Rose of a Sultan's Son

The Ladies of the Aristocracy

The Lady of a Grump

The Lady of a Sultan

The Wager of a Wallflower

Beyond the Aristocracy

The Pleasure of a Pirate

The Making of a Mistress

The Bride of a Baronet

The Caton of a Captain

Stella of Akrotiri

Origins

Deminon

Diana

The Lyon's Den (Dragonblade Publishing)

The Courage of a Lyon

The Lady of a Lyon

Note: Translations of select titles are available in German, Italian, Spanish and Portuguese.

CHAPTER 1
A SURE BET

April 1816, Weatherstone Manor, Mayfair

The moment Marcus Higgins, spare heir to the Earl of Greenley, invited Miss Lucy Fitzsimmons to join him in the Weatherstone Manor gardens during a ball was *the* defining moment in the young lady's life.

Or rather, it was the moment afterwards, when she said, "I'd be honored."

No. That isn't quite right. It was several minutes later. Enough time for them to make their way out of the French doors, along the path of pavers in the short clipped lawn, under the arbor adorned with climbing roses, and to the fountain featuring a statue of Cupid drawing his bow.

Say, ten minutes after the moment she said, "I'd be honored." For that was when Marcus told her she was the most lovely creature he had ever seen in his entire life.

Nervous, Lucy blinked and said, "I rather doubt that."

Apparently not used to someone countering his compliments, Marcus regarded her with a look of suspicion. "Why do you doubt my claim?"

"You only said it so you could steal a kiss," she challenged.

"I said it because it's true, and..." Here, he paused, as if realizing she had guessed correctly. "Well, yes, I admit it. I would like very much to kiss you."

Stunned he didn't deny her charge and even more stunned he still wished to kiss her, Lucy darted a glance in the direction from which they had come. Once her mother realized she wasn't in the ballroom or in the ladies retiring room, the woman would be on the hunt for her. They probably had five minutes until they were discovered.

Lucy leaned to one side and surveyed the part of the gardens directly behind where he stood, sure one of his friends from university was laying in wait to ambush them. No leaves rustled in the hedgerow, though. No suppressed chuckles sounded beyond the arbor.

Indecision had Lucy angling her head as she regarded Marcus Higgins with a curious expression. "Never once have you asked me to dance," she accused.

"This is the first ball I've ever attended in London," he said. At her look of doubt, he added, "I've been away at university. Before that..." He shrugged. "Living at Higgins House in Staffordshire."

Lucy decided he had a good excuse. "Oh," She

inhaled and let the breath out in a *whoosh*. A white cloud formed due to the chill in the air. In all the excitement, she hadn't realized how cold it was. "Well, then... before we do this, I wish to make a wager."

*M*arcus gave a start, his eyes rounding. "A wager?" He glanced around. Did she think that just because his father had been a well-known gambler, he was of the same persuasion? His own gambling had been limited to a few shillings over an occasional game of hazard at university. "What sort of wager?" He was about to add that he didn't have much in the way of blunt on his person, but then he noted she didn't carry a reticule, and he rather doubted she carried coins in her ballgown. Mayhap she had some banknotes stuffed down her stays?

He had to cease thinking about that possibility when his manhood reacted at the idea of him retrieving said bank notes from her person. His fingers had itched all night with the want to touch the tops of her rising moons, to trace the edge of the neckline of her bodice with a fingertip. He imagined her skin would be as soft as the velvet of her white ball gown. Warm and sweet as honey should his tongue delve into the space between those gorgeous breasts.

Hoping she didn't detect the sound of his groan of frustration given the splashing of falling water in the fountain, Marcus concentrated on Lucy's mouth. Her lips, more kissable than he had first realized, were moving.

"If anyone discovers we've done this, you'll have to marry me," Lucy stated. "I'm betting you won't."

He furrowed his dark brows, which had him appearing far older than his one-and-twenty years. "But... what do I get if I do? Marry you, I mean."

She blinked, apparently not expecting him to respond quite like that. "Well, *me*, I suppose. For *life*." She made this last sound entirely too ominous.

Marcus had to resist the urge to chuckle. He didn't want her thinking he was laughing at her when in fact he was more intrigued than he had been back in the ballroom. Having watched her dancing with a string of young—and not so young—gentlemen for most of the night, Marcus had come to the conclusion she was a happy young lady, free with her smiles and possessed of a musical laugh he wished to hear again and again.

But he had known that already.

He had known it for years.

Finding the young woman with hair the color of rich mahogany standing by herself between two of Lord Weatherstone's favorite potted palms had been the highlight of his evening.

So far.

He was hoping the kiss might be the new highlight.

"What do you stand to gain if I don't marry you?" he asked, more curious than serious with his query.

Lucy scoffed. "Besides a reputation as a ruined woman?" she replied, her chin rising in defiance. "You...

you have to pay me..." She seemed to quickly consider what amount of money might set her up for a comfortable life as a spinster. Surely more than the paltry dowry her brother claimed to have set aside on her behalf. "Ten thousand pounds," she announced.

"*What*?" he countered, realizing immediately he said the word far too loud. He leaned closer to her, his citrusy cologne mixing with the leafy green and earthy odors of the gardens to make for a heady scent. "First of all, no one is going to find out, because neither one of us is going to say anything about it," he reasoned. "I can keep a secret—"

"As can I," she quickly countered.

"So our kiss won't be discovered by anyone," he reasoned.

On the one hand, Lucy wished she could kiss and tell. She thought of all the friends—especially Marianne—with whom she could share the experience. Thought of all the ways she might describe touching lips with Marcus Higgins, spare heir to the Greenley earldom —no, make that the *current* heir to the Greenley earldom. His father had died earlier that year and his older brother, Max, was now the earl.

Keeping the news to herself was just as appealing, though. She'd be left displaying an enigmatic expression on her face for the rest of her life.

Marianne would simply think her daft.

"So you accept the terms?" she asked.

"I do," he replied, holding out his right hand.

Lucy regarded the appendage for a moment before sliding her gloved hand into it. Despite his gloves, she could tell he had long fingers. He gripped her hand in his —firmly—but not enough to crush her fingers as he gave her hand two shakes.

For a moment, they merely stared at one another, neither one of them moving. Then, all at once, his lips were on hers, a hand at her cheek as one of her gloved hands moved to the side of his neck.

There was a moment when Lucy was sure time stopped, for the sensation of the firm pillows of his lips pressed to hers was unlike anything she had experienced before. When he angled his head slightly and his hand urged her face to turn in the other direction, an entirely different sensation ensued.

A kiss. Not just a touching of lips or a quick peck, but an all-out, full-fledged, open-mouthed kiss that had her forgetting where she was and who she was with. Her fingers speared his dark hair as her body fell forward until her chest pressed to his.

She felt one of his arms wrap around the small of her back to pull her even closer. His tongue touched her teeth, and when she responded by touching his tongue with her own, she felt more than heard his growl of approval.

At some point, she might have mewled or moaned, or perhaps it was he who did so, for they slowly gave up their hold on one another and both stepped back in surprise.

Lucy blinked a few times.

He allowed a tentative grin.

About to say something—once she sorted what she might say to such an earth-shattering event—Lucy moved closer to him and froze when she realized they were no longer alone. An audible gasp sounded from their side of the arbor.

Drat!

Someone had discovered them.

They hadn't discussed *this* possibility.

"Why, Lucy Persephone Alexandra Fitzsimmons, whatever are you doing out here?"

Stiffening at the sound of her mother's voice, Lucy winced. Her eyes rounded when she realized the woman wasn't alone.

Lady Agnes Pettigrew was at her side.

Viscountess Agnes Pettigrew. The leading gossip maven of Mayfair. Despised by all but welcome in any parlor given the information she could provide on just about anyone in the peerage.

"Allow me," Marcus whispered.

"What?"

Marcus kept his gaze on Lucy as he said, "Despite the chill in the air, it is such a gorgeous evening, my ladies, I asked Miss Fitzsimmons if she might join me on a walk through the Earl's gardens." He finally turned to address Jane Burroughs Fitzsimmons, Viscountess Reardon, by bowing deeply and reaching for her silk-gloved hand. "Good evening, Lady Reardon." He turned and did the same with the viscountess.

"Lady Pettigrew. Your purple turban is most royal. You look as if you could be queen of your very own country."

The viscountess arched a graying brow, and the ostrich feather arcing out of her purple silk turban seemed to follow suit. "Greenley's whelp, are you not?" The query was said with a good deal of disgust, suggesting she thought him bad *ton*.

It was Marcus' turn to stiffen. He recognized the tone of voice. The sound of censure. The air of disgust, even if he hadn't been expecting to hear it from her.

As the second son of the late Maxwell Higgins, sixth Earl of Greenley, he had come to expect it during his short stay in London. Everyone in the *ton* seemed to think ill of Greenley. Despite his gaming on behalf of the Crown to help root out a band of foreign agents exporting large sums of British funds to France, the widowed Greenley couldn't tell anyone why it was he gambled to excess.

Unable to quit the habit, Marcus' father had been known as the Earl of Gaming until his death only a few months earlier. Without the Crown's funds to pay his bets, he had spent most of his time in a drunken stupor and died essentially broke.

At least Marcus had managed to secure his inheritance before it, too, was gambled away. With the help of his father's solicitor, he had established an account at the Bank of England and made arrangements for his immediate future the year prior.

An immediate future which did not include marriage.

He hadn't planned for that to occur for another two years.

As for Agnes Pettigrew's comment, it still surprised him. He had thought the viscountess an ally, not an enemy.

"I am the spare heir of the Greenley earldom, yes," Marcus admitted, his answer directed to both matrons.

"So you expect to gain my daughter's dowry by ruining her here in the—?"

"Mother!"

"No, my lady," Marcus stated, his offense apparent at hearing Lady Reardon's insinuation. "That was *not* my intention at all."

He was well aware of Lucy's sudden perusal of him. Despite the near dark of the gardens—the glow of a nearby Japanese lantern provided the only light on a moonless night—he could tell her eyes had narrowed with suspicion. "As I said, I merely wished to escort her through the gardens before I take my leave this evening."

He might have said more in his defense, except another couple was making their way through the rose arbor. Given Lady Reardon's rather loud voice, he realized if he didn't make a quick exit, the newcomers would learn of his foray with Lucy Fitzsimmons—if not from Lady Pettigrew, then surely from the viscountess.

"My apologies, but I must leave you," Marcus whispered, grabbing Lucy's hand to kiss the back of it. "I'll find you when I return." Without another word, he stepped behind Lucy and disappeared through the nearest hedgerow.

. . .

*L*ucy whirled around. She was about to call out for him but stifled the urge when she noticed another couple approaching, their soft murmurs broken up with titters and laughter.

Her mother had apparently noticed as well, for Lady Reardon huffed and said, "You're coming with me, young lady, and if you think I'm going to allow you to attend another ball this Season, why, just you wait until I tell your brother about this."

"Mother!" Lucy said in a hushed voice, sure the other couple was close enough to have heard the scold.

"Did he run off?" Lady Pettigrew asked in disgust, her skirts rustling as she stepped closer to the fountain in search of Marcus.

"Who?" Lucy asked, pretending innocence now that the older couple had joined them at the fountain.

Momentarily flustered, Lady Pettigrew didn't answer, and then she couldn't when Lord and Lady Weatherstone—their hosts for that evening's ball—greeted them.

"Lovely evening for a stroll," William, Earl of Weatherstone, remarked, snagging an ornate silver watch from his waistcoat pocket. "Except that it is rather chilly out here. So don't stay out here too long, my ladies. Supper is about to be served. At the stroke of midnight."

"We wouldn't miss it," Lady Reardon replied, her head—and enormous hairstyle—bending forward in greeting. For a moment, Lucy wondered if the entire coiffure was about to end up on the ground. She was sure it was a wig. Maybe more than one.

As for why her mother was even at the ball, Lucy supposed it was only because she had wished to go. Lady Reardon should by all accounts still be in mourning for her late husband and Lucy's father, Christopher Fitzsimmons, first Viscount Reardon. He had died only nine months prior, shortly before the wars with France ended.

At least Lady Reardon was dressed in a lavender gown, the color of half-mourning making her appear paler than usual.

"Why, we were just on our way back into the house," Lady Pettigrew added, her own head tipping to the side. The ostrich feather arced through the night air, and for the briefest of moments, Lucy wished a rather large bird might mistake it for its mate and settle atop the ridiculous turban.

Then she would have a story to tell. One she might use to negotiate a deal with the viscountess to keep quiet about the kiss she had shared with Marcus.

Although she wasn't completely sure Lady Pettigrew had paid witness to the kiss, she had to assume the woman would think she had. Given the viscountess' reputation as a gossip, Lucy was also sure she would be the topic of said gossip. For at least the next few days or so, her name would be spoken with a combination of horror and derision, censure and ridicule in every Mayfair parlor. From there, a notice would appear in the next issue of *The Tattler*, and thousands of Londoners would know of her indiscretion.

Lady L was caught engaging in a passionate kiss in Lord and Lady W's garden with none other than Lord G's spare heir. Will MH claim her dowry before the end of the Season? Only time will tell, but we're betting on it.

Lucy briefly wondered if she might take the bet. Surely *The Tattler* could afford a ten thousand pound payout.

For the entire Season, Lucy would be considered *persona non grata*, relegated to the end of ballrooms where the wallflowers mingled with potted palms whilst waiting for an occasional offer to dance.

Tempted to let tears flow and to claim she'd been duped into the kiss by Marcus Higgins, Lucy remembered her wager with him.

If anyone discovers we've done this, you'll have to marry me or pay me ten thousand pounds.

A sense of calm settled over Lucy as she and the two matrons made their way back to the ballroom.

If she was to play the part of a wallflower for the rest of the Season, she would do so as a wealthy woman.

She could hardly wait to tell Marianne.

CHAPTER 2
A POORLY TIMED
DEPARTURE

The following morning, London docks, Wapping

The fog was thick and the air chilly when the ancient Greenley town coach came to a stuttering halt well short of its destination. The trap door in the coach's ceiling opened, and the driver peered down into the dark interior.

"I daren't go farther, sir, lest the 'orses end up in the Thames." Despite the early hour, the docks were already crowded with cargo and crew, passengers and their trunks.

Marcus sighed. What else could possibly go wrong on this, his last day in London for at least two years? "It's all right, Carlson. We can walk from here," he called up. "But if you could find porters for our trunks—"

"Already done, sir. They are seeing to them right now." Even before he had finished his comment, the coach rocked slightly, an indication the trunks were being removed from their mounts on the back of the coach.

"I know I could use the walk," Franklin Turnbridge, brother of the current Earl of Fennington, said from the other bench. He yawned and cursed as one hand went to the side of his head. "Damned hangover. I can hardly wait to sleep it off on the boat."

"It's a ship," Marcus said by way of correction. "A clipper, I think." He hoped his traveling companion for his Grand Tour wouldn't develop seasickness. Unlike Marcus, Frank had stayed at the Weatherstone ball the night before until well past the supper, imbibing most of a bottle of brandy he had discovered in the card room. "Supposed to be the fastest means to Rome, if I'm to believe the shipping company."

The less time they spent en route to the Kingdom of the Two Sicilies to see the ancient Greek city-state sites and the historic Roman cities of Rome, Naples, Venice and Florence, the more time they would have for exploration. For meeting people. For drinking and carousing. For discovering the pleasures that could be had in the company of exotic ladies.

That last thought didn't hold as much appeal as it had when he had made the reservation for a cabin on *The Fairweather* the month prior. Back then, he was so relieved to learn he could afford to go on a Grand Tour, he had readily agreed to Frank's suggestion he join him for the itinerary his older brother, Felix, Earl of Fennington, had arranged on his behalf.

At some point, Marcus would have to discover how it

was the Fennington earldom could afford to underwrite Frank's trip, for rumors had abounded for several years their late father had left the earldom in dire straights.

Perhaps their similar circumstances were why it was Marcus and Frank had become such fast friends at university.

Glancing at his ticket for passage, Marcus remembered the agent's comment. If the weather favored them, they would make it to Rome in fifteen days.

Marcus hadn't considered the time of year when he and Frank had discussed a Grand Tour. Leaving in early spring meant forgoing most of the Season in London. They would be missing balls, *soirées* and *musicales*, routs and house parties, and all manner of garden parties—entertainments he had never been able to attend given they were always away for school.

Returning to London for a week's stay prior to his departure meant there was one opportunity to make an appearance at a *ton* ball, and Marcus had jumped at the chance.

His brother had no intention of going—Max was living in Staffordshire at Higgins House—so he had sent his acceptance in Max's stead and gone to the Weatherstone's ball the night before.

He had no expectations other than to enjoy a glass or two of champagne, play a game of whist in the card room, find a partner for a dance or two, and eat some of the midnight supper foods. When he'd had enough of the ball, he would head home to gather the last of his things, be off to collect Frank, then leave for the docks.

That is, until he saw *her* dancing with the Earl of Haddon. Until he heard her giggling with two of her friends as they surreptitiously drank champagne. Until he watched her flirt with a young buck.

Lucy Fitzsimmons. The love of his life since he'd been a young boy.

He knew he had to have her. Knew he had to claim her as his own. Knew he had to change the entire trajectory of his future to make it so.

The kiss in the gardens was only the beginning.

For a fleeting moment during their kiss, he had entertained the thought he might give Frank his apologies and simply remain in London to court Miss Lucy.

Not that he really needed to court her. At least, not now. They had been discovered kissing, which meant the terms of the wager were to be paid.

If anyone discovers we've done this, you'll have to marry me or pay me ten thousand pounds.

Since he didn't have ten thousand pounds—at least, not yet—he would have to marry Lucy, which was just fine with him.

As soon as he was settled in his cabin on *The Fairweather,* he would write her a letter explaining his intentions. Ask that she wait for him—she was probably too young to marry now anyway—and he would see to their union when he returned.

By then, the blunt he had invested in a canal project up north might begin paying dividends. Gregory Grandby had suggested it would be probable. The cousin of Milton, Earl of Torrington, and grandson of a duke on one side and an earl on the other, Grandby had his offices in Oxford Street. He had earned a reputation for choosing investment projects that paid handsomely—as long as an investor could be patient.

Marcus could afford to be patient. He had enough blunt set aside to not only go on the Grand Tour for two years, but also enough to live a few years more without an income.

"Is this it?" Frank asked, interrupting Marcus' reverie.

Glancing at the stern of the ship, Marcus recognized the name. "She is *The Fairweather*," he confirmed.

With one last glance in the direction of London, he climbed the gangway and followed the directions to his cabin.

He had a letter to write.

CHAPTER 3
A BROTHER'S CONDITION CONCERNS

Later that morning, Reardon Manor, Mayfair

Having found the breakfast parlor empty, a relieved Lucy settled into her usual chair at the round table and watched as a footman delivered a cup of tea, coddled eggs, toast points, and a rasher of bacon with a haste she hadn't witnessed before.

"Smithers, whatever is wrong?" she asked.

The rather tall, lean servant paused near the door. "I'm needed upstairs, my lady," he replied. "Your brother..." Here he stopped, his dark brows furrowed in confusion. "Well, you're probably already aware."

Lucy half-stood from her chair. "What? What is it?"

Smithers' eyes rounded. "He's not doing so well on this morning. A bit deep in his cups last evenin'."

Blinking, Lucy settled back into her chair. "Oh," she murmured, tucking into her meal. "Is that all?" This last was said with a roll of her eyes. Her mother had no doubt told him about finding her with Marcus Higgins when they returned from the ball at one o'clock that morning. He had probably drunk an entire bottle of brandy in response.

Although Christopher Fitzsimmons, the second Viscount Reardon, had joined them for the start of the Weatherstone's ball, he had left the affair well before supper was served, complaining of heartburn. The news of her indiscretion with Marcus had probably only worsened his symptoms.

Well, she wasn't about to take all the blame for something for which she was only half responsible. There were two people kissing under the watchful eyes of Cupid in Lord Weatherstone's gardens last night, and Marcus Higgins was one of them.

The cur.

The wretch.

The scoundrel.

The rake.

The insufferable second son of a gambler.

Lucy choked down her third toast point, continuing to fume over the sudden disappearance of her cohort in her first kiss.

Once again, the thought of that kiss had her audibly sighing. Could there ever be anything else so wonderful in life as that kiss? Everything about it had been awe-inspiring.

The firm pillows of his lips.

The taste of champagne.

The scents of amber and citrus and musk.

The sensation of his tongue tangling with hers.

The way his hand caressed her jaw, sending delightful shivers beneath her skin.

The feel of his warm breath on her cheek.

The sight of his dark lashes resting on the tops of his cheekbones before she'd been forced to close her own eyes.

The hard planes of his chest where her hands had rested against it.

Even now, her breasts felt heavy and swollen, her nipples hard behind her stays.

What would it feel like for his lips to kiss them? she wondered. To be licked and suckled and flicked with the thumb he had brushed along her jaw.

Her entire body shuddered as frissons danced under her skin and through her belly to the space at the top of her thighs.

She felt the sudden dampness and wondered what was happening to her.

Desire had her wishing Marcus Higgins was with her. He needed to do whatever it was that came after a kiss. Whatever was necessary to relieve the throbbing ache. To sooth her heated skin. To quell her pebbled nipples. To put her to rights.

Where was her god of lust when she needed him?

The sound of the butler answering the front door had her pushing away from the table. Perhaps Marcus knew of her discomfort well before receiving the note she had given her lady's maid. Persimmon had promised she would see to its delivery, claiming she knew of a maid next door who knew someone who worked in Pendleton House, home of the late Earl of Greenley.

A hint of panic had her wondering where she might hide Marcus once he was in the house. Perhaps they could make it to one of the guest bedchambers. There they could engage in kisses without fear of interruption. Engage in all manner of whatever else came after a kiss.

Surely Marcus would know what to do. He was older. He had been away at university. He had probably done whatever it was men did after such scorching kisses with a number of women.

A sudden wave of jealousy coupled with indignation had her experiencing a moment of indigestion.

She empathized with her brother.

Lucy made it to the door of the breakfast parlor and was about to step into the hall when the butler, Peters, hurried past, followed by a black-clad man carrying a valise.

She recognized him. Dr. Fortnum. Her brother's physician.

A quick glance around the hall had her noticing a distinct lack of household maids. The house seemed entirely too quiet.

Climbing the stairs with the intention of going to her bedchamber, she instead stopped outside her brother's master suite. Peeking inside, her eyes rounded at seeing the physician bending over the bed, administering something sweet-smelling, the odor so strong she was reminded of Lady Morganfield's garden.

Laudanum.

"Is Christopher going to be all right?" she asked once her mother took note of her presence. The young man was only three-and-twenty. Despite his youth, he had shown valor during a particularly bloody battle the year prior—like his father before him, he had even suffered a bullet wound to his middle. Lucy was fairly sure her uncle, Matthew Fitzsimmons, Viscount Chamberlain and head of the Foreign Office, had something to do with his brother's reward of the Reardon viscountcy by the king.

"I'll be fine," Christopher said, pushing away the doctor's attempt to make him take a second spoonful of the medication.

"I never should have told you about what happened last night," Jane said, a handkerchief gripped so tightly in one hand, Lucy feared the laundress would never be able to iron out the wrinkles. The skirt of the gray gown she wore showed evidence of her nervous habit of pleating the fabric between her fingers. She had probably been doing it all morning until the physician arrived.

Christopher barked out a laugh. "Oh, Mother, my current condition has absolutely *nothing* to do with Lucy and her foray into the gardens," he claimed, straightening on the bed. "I've merely had heartburn since last night's dinner." He waved away the physician, who busied himself with the contents of his valise. "Now, Sister, tell me everything." He crooked a finger in Lucy's direction, summoning her to step closer.

"Everything?" Lucy repeated, a look of horror crossing her face. "About what?"

To her relief, Dr. Fortnum nodded to her brother and

took his leave, the butler joining him once he was out in the corridor. Now only her mother and brother were in the master bedchamber.

"You're sure it was Marcus Higgins who kissed you?"

Lucy scoffed. "Who said he kissed me?" she countered defiantly.

Her mother aimed a scowl in her direction. "Lady Pettigrew was quite insistent that she saw you in an embrace with the boy."

"Only because she wants a tidbit of gossip to share," Christopher put in, which had both women staring at him in surprise. He shrugged. "I am well aware the crone is a gossip monger," he added. "*The Tattler* probably pays her for it."

"So it doesn't matter if I did or didn't kiss Marcus Higgins," Lucy argued. "Either way, she'll claim I did, and my reputation will be ruined."

Christopher exchanged a quick look with their mother. "Possibly," he hedged.

"*Probably*," Jane insisted. "Perhaps we can send you to live at the dowager cottage in Somerset? With a relative, of course," she suggested.

"What?" Lucy's eyes were wide with fright.

"You could attend balls in the Upper Rooms in Bath and enjoy the elegant stupidity of all the private parties," her mother went on, apparently warming to the idea of sending her away.

"Mother, we're not sending Lucy to live in Bath," Christopher stated.

"Well, it's just an idea," Jane countered. Her attention

was captured by the butler, who had returned to the doorway. "What is it, Peters?"

"You have a caller, my lady. Viscountess Pettigrew." A wince crossed his face at the same moment his nose wrinkled, as if he had sniffed an especially offensive odor. Probably the laudanum. "I put her in the downstairs salon."

Jane exchanged a glance of frustration with her children before taking her leave of Christopher's bedchamber.

Moving to take her mother's place closer to Christopher, Lucy whispered, "My reputation is most definitely ruined." She let out a long sigh. "I was with him. Next to a fountain."

"The one with Cupid?" Christopher asked with a crooked grin. Another moment, and the grin had grown into a huge smile. He was enjoying himself far too much. "Through the rose arbor?"

She rolled her eyes. "I don't know. I wasn't looking at the..." She clamped her mouth shut and sighed again, wondering if her brother might have kissed his betrothed, Lady Maria, next to that very same fountain the year prior. "Well, all is not lost, I suppose," she murmured.

Her brother sat up, his disheveled hair making him appear as if he'd had a rough night. "What have you done?" There was a glint in his eye suggesting he knew there was more to the story than what his mother had told him earlier.

"Nothing," Lucy replied. Upon seeing his arched

brow, she huffed. "I merely ensured there would be some *recompense* should we be discovered together before I allowed anything to happen."

His eyes narrowing, her brother asked, "Recompense? How much?"

"He has to pay me ten thousand pounds."

His bark of laughter could probably be heard all the way downstairs and into the front salon. "Marcus Higgins hasn't got *ten* pounds," he said. "His father was broke when he died, and everyone knows it."

"We shook on it," she countered, her mouth dropping open in dismay.

Seeing his sister's expression, Christopher quickly sobered. "And if you weren't discovered?" he prompted.

"If we weren't discovered?" she repeated in confusion.

"What would he owe you?"

Her eyes widened. "Oh. Uh... well, nothing. Just the kiss, I suppose."

Christopher sat back into the stack of pillows and stared at her with a most curious expression.

"What is it?" she asked.

He shrugged. "I'm still shocked you think he's going to pay you ten thousand pounds."

Tempted to punch him in the shoulder, Lucy huffed. Before she could say anything, her brother held up his hands as if to ward off a blow.

"Was this some sort of wager?" he asked.

She stiffened. "And if I say it was?"

He shrugged. "It's rather clever. Either way, *he's* the one who got stuck with paying the bill."

Lucy's hands went to her hips. "What's *that* supposed to mean?"

"What did you stand to lose either way?" he countered.

She considered the query. "My reputation, if you must know, which is about to be in tatters the very moment Lady Pettigrew begins paying her calls today."

Christopher merely grinned in response.

"*He's* the one who wanted to kiss *me*," she argued.

He continued to grin. "Says the girl who willingly joined him in the gardens."

Lucy huffed out a breath. "I admit I was... flattered," she murmured.

"And?" he prompted.

Her eyes darted to the side before she whispered. "It was quite lovely." Lucy had a thought she had never seen her brother's eyebrows climb so high on his forehead before. "Well, it was," she added lamely.

"So... you would do it again? With Marcus Higgins?"

She sighed contentedly and nodded. "Was it like that for you? Kissing Maria, I mean?"

Christopher inhaled, and his up-until-then paleness was quickly replaced with a good deal of color. "That's none of your concern."

Scoffing, she argued, "That's not fair. You must have kissed your betrothed."

For a moment, she wished she hadn't mentioned the word "betrothed," for whenever the topic of Christopher's choice for a bride came up, his face shuttered and he refused to speak. If their mother had been in the room, she would have made sure to put voice to her distrust of the Spanish aristocrat's daughter he had gifted with a ring the year before.

So Lucy was surprised when her brother responded.

"Of course I have kissed Maria," he claimed. "However, I'm not about to kiss and tell. At least, not to anyone else. And neither should you. Not even Marianne," he warned.

Lucy inhaled to respond but quickly realized he was right. Well, except for Marianne. Lucy had every intention of telling Marianne because, well, Lady Pettigrew had probably shared her news from last night with her lady's maid and everyone else in her household and would continue doing so in every parlor she paid a call on that afternoon.

How many parlors could that be? Two? Three? Ten?

He reached out and chucked her chin. "I almost feel sorry for you."

"Why?" she countered in surprise.

"Lucy," he said in his most serious voice. "You're about to experience the worst Season of your life. Once words gets out, you'll be lucky to receive any invitations to parlors let alone offers to dance at balls," he explained. "I never thought I'd say this about you, but you're about to become a... a *wallflower*."

Lucy swallowed. Hard. She blinked, not realizing she did so to stave off tears. "How can you say that? How can you be so *cruel*?"

He furrowed his brows and gave his head a shake. "I'm older than you. I've seen it happen to the very best of young ladies." He sighed and suddenly lifted his head.

When he didn't say anything else for a time, Lucy finally asked, "What is it?"

"My heartburn. It's gone," he claimed as a smile split his lips. "Thanks to you, I think," he added with a grin.

Lucy pulled one of the pillows from behind him and hit him with it. She might have continued doing so, but she no longer had the energy to do so.

She took her leave of her brother's bedchamber as the tears began to fall.

Christopher watched her go, his momentary humor replaced with the melancholy he had been experiencing ever since his return from the Continent the year before.

Why hadn't he heard from Maria? He was sure they had parted on good terms. She wore his ring. She had a copy of their marriage certificate. Her father should have brought her back to England once the war with France was over.

Ten months have passed, he thought in dismay. The last time he had seen her was the day before he was dispatched to the Continent. A day that had him assuming his duties as a captain in the British Army. A week later, he and his troops were assigned to one of the coalition armies that would eventually end Napoleon's reign as emperor of France.

He winced at the thought that the brandy he and his father had shared the night before his departure had been their last together. Only a few days later, Christopher Fitzsimmons, first Viscount Reardon, succumbed to a sudden fever, dying as his wife and daughter stood by his bedside.

Meanwhile, the final battle against Napoleon at Waterloo had nearly been the end of Christopher.

He absently rubbed the area where a bullet had penetrated his mid-section, the wound still giving him trouble on occasion. He couldn't be too upset with his mother's overreaction to his heartburn, although Fortnum's insistence he swallow laudanum wasn't welcome.

At least his heartburn was gone, though.

His thoughts once again went to Maria.

Lady Maria Paloma Silvestri y Arístegui de Benavides.

He chuckled softly at the memory of how long it had taken him to learn how to say her entire name. How when he had first made love to her, he had recited it twice before he took her virtue.

Where are you, Maria?

He was sure she was looking forward to a life with him when she and her father, the Conde of Albacete, said their farewells. He had married her, after all. She had even whispered a vow that she would love him forever, her gloved hand cupping his ear as her lips spoke the words that had sustained him for months while he recovered from his wound.

So why hadn't she responded to any of his letters?

Knowing his mother had not been pleased at the

prospect of him taking a Spanish nobleman's daughter to wife, he had suspected she might be intercepting his correspondence. However, Peters had assured him nothing had come for him from Spain or anywhere else on the Continent.

One of his recent missives to her had been returned, a note in Spanish indicating no one lived at the address he had written on the envelope. If she and her father had taken up residence somewhere else besides in Madrid, he had no way of knowing where that might be.

He was fairly sure there was someone who might know of her whereabouts, but Christopher would have to pay a call at his uncle's office to learn more.

"Peters!" he called out, rising from his bed.

The butler appeared at the bedchamber's door a moment later. "My lord?"

"Have the town coach made ready," he ordered. "I need to go to Whitehall."

"Right away, my lord."

Christopher watched him go and then hurried to dress. Surely Matthew Fitzsimmons, Viscount Chamberlain and the head of the Foreign Office, would know the whereabouts of a certain spy he employed.

CHAPTER 4
DISPATCHING A LETTER

eanwhile, on The Fairweather

Once their trunks and valises had been delivered to their cabin on *The Fairweather*, the two recent graduates of Cambridge University realized their quarters might be too cramped to live in during the voyage to Rome. Besides the two bunks, one mounted above the other on one wall, the cabin featured a square table, two wooden chairs, and a lantern. Their luggage took up nearly all the remaining floor space.

"I'm going to bed," Frank announced, shedding his top coat before he deftly jumped up and onto the top bunk.

"Hey," Marcus said in protest, expecting he would take the top bunk. A thought he might be tossed out of it in the event of bad weather had him reconsidering.

"Wake me when the food is served."

The reminder they hadn't eaten breakfast prior to their departure that morning had Marcus' stomach growling in protest. He acknowledged Frank's request as he hung his top hat on a peg. "Captain St. John said we could join him for meals," he commented. "Sinclair and Hornsby as well," he added, referring to two other classmates who had boarded *The Fairweather* for the trip to Rome and their Grand Tours.

He had been relieved upon meeting the older captain in the wheelhouse. Half expecting a piratical character sporting a peg leg, Marcus was pleased when John St. John proved nothing of the sort.

He had obviously been a sea captain for some time. For the past three years, he had sailed the London to Rome to London route as captain of *The Fairweather*, although he hinted he'd had other responsibilities on the side. His crew seemed loyal, especially his first mate, a man he called Rodney.

Although the ship had been beset by the same sorts of disasters any sailing ship did, *The Fairweather* seemed in good shape. Even though steam ships were taking over most of the work of moving goods across the water, the sailing vessels were still in demand for their speed in seas where winds could be relied upon to fill their sails.

Marcus opened his trunk and pulled out his stationery box. Moving to the table, he took a seat and considered how to compose a letter to the woman who would one day be his wife.

Dear Sweeting,

He scratched his chin. Perhaps it was too soon for

endearments. Lucy was probably still suffering her mother's scolds.

Dear Gorgeous,

Rolling his eyes, he could just imagine how Lucy would roll hers upon reading the salutation.

Dear Miss Fitzsimmons,

Yes, it was ordinary, but it showed he knew her name, and it showed a level of respect she deserved.

Dear Miss Fitzsimmons,
I owe you an apology for what happened last night, although...

He sat back. An apology implied he was sorry when he really wasn't. How could he be when their kiss had been so earth-shattering?

Their intimate act had been somewhat of a surprise. One of those serendipitous events that could change the course of one's life.

The kiss would certainly change theirs. Or rather, the discovery by Lady Pettigrew would. The hag had been lying in wait to follow an unsuspecting couple into the gardens for the sole purpose of creating a gossip-worthy event.

He had seen to it. But not in the manner it had actually occurred. How could Lady Pettigrew betray him with her cutting words?

Giving his head a shake, Marcus returned his attention to the letter.

Although I must admit, I am not sorry for having kissed you. I found the experience most illuminating, for it opened my eyes to the possibility of what is to come in my life. Of what I may look forward to for the rest of my life.

I do hope you are able to see it the same.

Here he paused and tried to imagine Lucy's reaction. Either she would be of the same mind as him, or she wouldn't. Perhaps she would require some prodding.

As per our agreement, I will of course marry you. I look forward to the day when we will say our vows and take up residence in Pendleton House in Mayfair.

It wasn't as if anyone else lived in Pendleton House. The butler there claimed ignorance as to the whereabouts of his older sister, Barbara. His younger sister was living with an aunt in Staffordshire. If his older brother remained in Staffordshire at the Greenley country estate, Higgins House, then Lucy would be the lady of Pendleton House. Was that enough of an incentive in the event merely marrying him wasn't?

He jerked himself out of his reverie and continued to write.

There is a slight matter of timing, however. I have only this morning boarded a sailing vessel bound for Rome as I have embarked on my Grand Tour. Frank Turnbridge and I made the arrangements well before our terms at Cambridge ended a fortnight ago. The itinerary will keep us away from British shores for two years.

Upon my return, I shall pay a call to renew our acquaintance so that a date can be set for our wedding. I do hope this will not inconvenience you. It will give you two years to attend the entertainments of the ton with the knowledge you no longer need to impress a young man into proposing marriage.

Let this letter be a formal acknowledgment of our betrothal. Upon my return to British shores, I will see to paying a call at Reardon Manor to seek your brother's permission to marry you.

Please know that I shall think about you often as I visit Ancient Greek temples, for I know it was Cupid who was responsible for our meeting again.

Yours in service,

Marcus Higgins

Marcus set aside his pen and reread the letter, grunting softly as he imagined how she might react upon reading the news of his departure.

He briefly thought about adding "Heir to the Greenley earldom," at the bottom, but thought better of it.

About to write a post scriptum to mention he would

write again soon, he couldn't when the ship suddenly jerked and the quick steps and shouts of sailors sounded from above.

"What's going on?" he asked aloud.

From the upper bunk where he had a clear view through the room's only porthole window, Frank said, "They're undoing the ropes from the dock."

"Already?" Marcus hurriedly folded the letter and addressed it. "Dammit. I thought I'd have more time," he murmured, rushing from the room to climb the companionway.

When he landed on the deck, he had to quickly step aside or fall backward given the sailor who nearly collided with him. A sail unfurled on the fore-mast followed by another on the main-mast. The sense of sudden motion he felt was confirmed when he realized they were no longer tethered to the dock.

Once he was sure he wasn't in anyone's way, he rushed to the railing in search of anyone on the dock he might engage in the delivery of his letter.

Spotting a young man dressed in the uniform of a porter, he called out to him.

The porter looked up. "Aye?" He stutter-stepped into motion, matching the ship's movement along the dock.

"Can you see to delivering this letter?" Marcus called out as he held up the envelope. He frowned when he realized the ship was moving faster than he thought.

The porter looked both ways and began jogging in the same direction as *The Fairweather*. "Toss it, sir," he called out. "I'll see what I can do!"

Marcus hoisted the envelope and gave it his best throw. Although the envelope landed well away from the porter, it did land on the dock. "For your trouble," Marcus called out as he tossed a sovereign.

This time, the porter caught the silver coin and held it up. "Good travels, sir."

Marcus watched as the porter picked up the envelope and seemed to study the address, but the foggy and crowded docks soon hid him from view as *The Fairweather* increased its easterly movement on the Thames. Within the hour, they would be in the Channel and headed for the Strait of Gibraltar.

He hoped his missive might end up in Lucy's hands well before then.

CHAPTER 5
YOUNG LADIES
COMMISERATE

*L*ater that day, Reardon Manor, Mayfair

"What do you mean, he wasn't there?" Lucy asked when her maid relayed the message she had been waiting for most of the day.

Persimmon shrugged her shoulders. "Perkins spoke with the kitchen maid at Pendleton House," she said, referring to one of the footmen who was frequently dispatched with messages. "She said the young man was there yesterday. He left last night for an entertainment and was not in the household this morning for breakfast. Mr. Higgins was not expected for dinner this evening, either."

Lucy rolled her eyes. "He was at the Weatherstone's ball last evening," she insisted, not adding that he had not only stolen a kiss but had accepted her wager. His quick departure after Lady Pettigrew—and her mother—had appeared at the fountain had been rather odd. Cowardly, even.

"Perhaps he had to return to university," Persimmon suggested, moving to undo the pins in Lucy's hair so she could do a different hairstyle for that night's dinner.

"I rather doubt it," Lucy murmured. For a moment, she imagined him at a gaming hell, playing hazard or hand after hand of faro, losing the money he owed her.

Ten thousand pounds.

After that afternoon's tea in her mother's parlor, it was evident she was not going to have a successful Season. Lady Pettigrew had already spread her news about her supposed discovery on her morning calls. By the time she appeared in Lady Reardon's parlor at half-past three o'clock, hinting that Lucy had been discovered with a rake in the gardens near the fountain featuring the statue of Cupid, the damage had been done.

Lucy's reputation was in tatters.

She'll be forced to take her place among the wallflowers at all the balls this Season, Lady Pettigrew had said with feigned sadness.

As if Lucy wasn't sitting ten feet away, her face bright red with embarrassment.

What could she say in her own defense?

"Oh, I'm quite sure you have me confused with someone else," came to mind, but of course it didn't do so until ten minutes after the ladies had taken their leave of her mother's parlor.

Damnation!

How many other parlors had Lady Pettigrew been in this afternoon?

After a moment of near-panic, Lucy asked, "Did he

leave my note with someone at Pendleton House?"

"The butler, I believe," Persimmon murmured.

Lucy cursed under her breath. The butler would merely pass it onto Lord Greenley, and from there, who knew what would happen to it? Did the current Earl of Greenley spend his days deep in his cups or at a gaming hell like his father had? If he was sober enough to decipher her note, what would he think? Did he even know his spare heir had made the wager? That he owed her ten thousand pounds?

Or marriage.

Not that she ever expected Marcus Higgins to marry her. No. He would pay her ten thousand pounds so he wouldn't have to marry her.

The cur.

The scoundrel.

The rake.

The sound of a clearing throat had her glancing at the dressing table mirror to see the reflection of Peters standing at the open door to her bedchamber. "What is it?" she asked, not intending for annoyance to sound in her voice.

Peters' expression of boredom changed to a frown. "Miss Marianne has paid a call, Miss Fitzsimmons."

A sense of relief settled over Lucy at hearing her best friend had arrived. She had no doubt learned of Lucy's fate in her mother's parlor. "Oh, do send her up," she said, hoping her relief was apparent. She glanced at Persimmon's reflection. "How much longer do you think?"

"Two more pins, my lady," the lady's maid responded, twirling a lock of hair close to the crown of her head. Lucy was sure if her hair was pulled any tighter, her eyebrows would appear as if she was permanently surprised.

Surely it was an appropriate reaction to learning what the entire *ton* was thinking of her.

"I'll see to undressing myself after dinner," she said as she watched Persimmon finish the coiffure.

"Very good, my lady." Persimmon poked a series of gem-topped pins into the seam of the top knot, the green paste stones a close match to the dinner gown Lucy wore. "I'll see you in the morning." She curtsied and took her leave at the same moment Marianne Harkinson appeared at the door.

"You're looking especially lovely this evening," Marianne remarked, tossing a reticule onto Lucy's bed before she unceremoniously joined it and lay back with her arms spread wide.

"I wish I felt like it," Lucy groused.

"So... what's it like to be 'thoroughly and most decidedly ruined'?" her friend teased.

Jerking her head around to regard Marianne with a look of shock, Lucy scoffed. "So you already heard?" She shouldn't be surprised.

Marianne rolled her eyes. "*You* are the talk of the town. And you'll be the featured topic of an article in *The Tattler*, if Lady Pettigrew is to be believed."

Groaning, Lucy joined her friend on the bed. Ignoring how her gown might suffer, she lay back and stared up at the fabric of the canopy above. "She didn't even pay witness to it," she blurted.

Marianne glanced over at her. "Pay witness to what?"

"The kiss."

Her eyes rounding, Marianne sat up. "So it's... it's true? You *were* with Marcus Higgins in the Weatherstone gardens last night?" Her mouth dropped open. "You *kissed* him?"

Lucy stayed prone and scoffed. "He kissed *me*," she countered, deciding she could tell her best friend. Everyone else seemed to know, even if it wasn't because Lady Pettigrew had actually paid witness to her transgression.

The woman had merely guessed correctly.

"You *allowed* him to do so?" Marianne asked. Her query came out sounding more as if she might be in awe rather than in shock.

Indeed Lucy had, but not right away. Not until she had some sort of assurances. Not until the wager had been accepted. "I did. But not like that," she admitted in a whisper.

"What were you doing *before* he kissed you?" Marianne matched her conspiratorial whisper.

"Making a wager. Which I won, I might add." Before Marianne could ask the details, Lucy sat up and added, "If we were discovered, he either had to pay me ten thousand pounds or marry me."

Marianne blinked several times. "So... when is the wedding?"

Lucy scoffed once more and fell back onto the bed.

"What makes you think I have any intention of marrying Marcus Higgins?"

It was Marianne's turn to scoff. "Everyone knows Marcus doesn't have ten thousand pounds," she reasoned.

Lucy winced. Now where had she heard *that* before? "Well, he accepted the terms of the wager, and now that Lady Pettigrew claims to have seen something she did not, he owes me."

Settling back onto the bed, Marianne's expression turned thoughtful. "Were you two discovered together? She said you were by the statue of Cupid."

"We were there," Lucy admitted, her body warming at the memory. "But the kissing had already ended by the time she showed up with Mother."

"Were you… touching him?" Marianne's eyes rounded. "Was he touching you?"

Lucy winced. "No! As I recall, we had stepped away from one another because we heard someone approaching. So no, we were not in some sort of compromising position." A grimace crossed her face. "But we were alone."

The way Marianne quieted had Lucy regarding her with a curious expression. "What?"

The other girl shrugged. "It seems rather odd that he would do such a thing the night before he left on his Grand Tour."

Lucy sat up so fast, she let out an "ouch" when her neck made an unnatural sound. "What's this?"

Marianne regarded her friend with a curious expression. "Marcus left this morning with Frank Turnbridge," she explained, her words sounding as if they were said from far away. She let out a long sigh. "They're off to Rome and then to Sicily and Greece."

Anger replaced Lucy's annoyance. "And you know this how?" The look of guilt on Marianne's face had Lucy furrowing her brows. "Marianne? You look positively..."

Lucy didn't finish the accusation as she regarded her friend in shock. However would Marianne know the second son of the Earl of Fennington had left England with Marcus?

Unless...

"You and... you and *Frank*?" she whispered in shock. Her eyes widened even more. "Last night... when Marcus asked me to join him in the gardens... you... you and Frank were dancing, were you not?"

Marianne swallowed. "In a manner of speaking, yes."

"Marianne..."

"Oh, all right. I *was* with Frank. In the gardens. Behind a hedgerow. Not far from you, in fact, if you were indeed at the fountain," Marianne admitted.

Lucy clasped a hand over her mouth to stifle her scold. Stepping back, she wrapped her other arm around her middle and simply stared at her friend.

Marianne winced. "I came to tell you. I was going to tell you last night, but I couldn't find you at supper—"

"Mother had me in the coach and on our way home when supper was served," Lucy explained. "I still have to send a note of apology to Lord Haddon. I promised him the last waltz since I finally have my special dispensation from Almack's to do so," she added on a sigh. "So... you two kissed?"

Marianne allowed a wan smile as her face displayed a pink blush. "We did. And it wasn't the first time."

Lucy sat on the bed next to Marianne. Hard. "You've been kissing Turnbridge, and you didn't tell me?" she asked, her voice filled with disappointment.

"I couldn't," her friend said, her shaking head sending the ringlets at her temples into a frenzy. "I promised I wouldn't tell anyone," she added in a plaintive tone. "Now that he's gone on his Grand Tour..." She shrugged. "I needed to tell *someone*."

Lucy understood her friend's wistful comment. "What sort of wager did you make with Mr. Turnbridge?"

Marianne held up her right hand. At the base of her fourth finger was a band of gold with a red gemstone mounted on it.

Her eyes widening in shock, Lucy grabbed Marianne's hand and brought it closer. "He *gave* this to you?"

Nodding, Marianne said, "After he proposed marriage." Her grin broadened. "We're to wed when he returns from the Mediterranean."

"Which will be...?"

"In two years," she said. "He told me he wanted to be sure I didn't consider anyone else's suit whilst he was on his trip. Not that I would," Marianne quickly added. "I've held a candle for Frank for... well, you know," she murmured as she rolled her eyes.

Lucy gave a start. If she knew, she wouldn't feel such

shock at hearing the news. "Have you two discussed marriage in the past?" she asked, not bothering to hide her dismay.

Her best friend was betrothed. Well, she could be considered betrothed as well if Marcus didn't come up with ten thousand pounds.

Screwing her face into a grimace, Marianne seemed to think on the query before she said, "When we were four or five, I think it was." She brightened. "And then again last year. The night of my come-out, he reminded me. I thought he was teasing me, but he wasn't."

Lucy scoffed. "You didn't tell me any of this," she complained.

"Because I promised I wouldn't."

"But why?"

Marianne sighed. "He's a second son. Like Marcus, he has to rely on his brother for an allowance, and until last year, he wasn't sure of the Fennington earldom's financial situation." She lifted a shoulder. "Apparently he spoke with Father yesterday."

"He asked his permission?"

"Well, of course," Marianne replied. "Father pulled me into his study and said he'd given his permission but with a caveat."

"A condition?" Lucy queried.

Marianne lowered her voice to a whisper. "Yes. My mother is not to learn of it. At least, not until Frank returns from his trip."

Lucy boggled. "But, why not? Won't she be thrilled to learn you're betrothed?" Like most mothers of daughters of an age to marry, Persephone Harkinson was forever bringing up possible matches for Marianne whilst they enjoyed tea in her parlor.

Marianne tittered. "My Father takes great joy in vexing Mother. Every time she brings up the topic of a potential suitor for me, he tells her I'm too young to wed and that he'll see to a match for me." She covered her mouth with a hand as she giggled. "He seemed quite pleased with himself yesterday, as if he was the cat who swallowed the canary, so I rather doubt he'll be able to keep the news to himself for two whole years."

Herbert Harkinson, Baron Harkinson, was known for his good humor and quick wit, so this last didn't surprise Lucy too much. She might even have found humor in the situation if her own brother showed the least bit of interest in her future husband.

"So, you mustn't say a word to anyone," Marianne said.

"Oh, I won't. It will be our secret." She paused as she considered her own dilemma. "The same must be said for my situation as well, though."

Marianne furrowed a brow. "But... you were caught. It's not exactly a secret."

"I was referring to the terms of the wager," Lucy argued.

"Oh."

Lucy dipped her head. "So... what changed to allow Turnbridge to propose?"

Marianne's face lit up in delight. "He wrested his inheritance from his older brother," she replied. "He is using some of it for the trip, but most of it he has given to a man named Mr. Grandby. To invest on his behalf," she explained. "He's a cousin to Lord Torrington and is apparently very good at making money for his clients."

"Apparently?" Lucy repeated, a look of fright replacing her curious expression. Suspicion had her asking, "What if he's a shyster?"

Her friend shook her head. "I asked Father about him," Marianne countered. "I don't think I've seen him look so surprised at hearing one of my questions in my entire life."

"Surprised horrified, or surprised...?"

"He was *impressed* with me," Marianne claimed, lifting her chin. "Asked me how I knew of the gentleman and wondered if I intended to ask for my dowry so I could invest it."

Lucy gave a start. "What did you tell him?"

Marianne grinned. "I told him my betrothed had invested with the gentleman, and I would allow him to decide if my dowry should be invested as well."

Lucy gasped. "Had Turnbridge already asked your father for your hand? Before you told him about the investment?"

Marianne furrowed a brow. "I don't think so," she hedged. "But he seemed quite happy to learn of the arrangement. That's when we agreed not to tell Mother."

"Surely she's noticed your ring," Lucy countered. She had to admit she might not have noticed it if Marianne hadn't pointed it out to her, but surely the girl's mother would.

"I hide it in my pocket when I'm with her."

Wincing, Lucy could just imagine Baroness Harkinson's reaction upon learning her only daughter was betrothed to the second son of an earl. "You will have a vinaigrette on your person when you tell her, I hope," she murmured.

Marianne giggled. "My Father said the very same thing."

For a moment, Lucy merely stared at Marianne's ring, a streak of jealousy making it difficult to be happy for her friend. Even if she had to wait two years for Frank Turnbridge to return to British shores, Marianne already knew what her future held.

Lucy now wished she was more certain of her own.

"I must get home," Marianne announced suddenly. "We have the Huntington ball tonight," she said.

Rolling her eyes, Lucy stared up at her canopy. "Probably my last ball before I'm a confirmed wallflower," she replied. "And two years before I can take my revenge."

Although Marianne didn't say anything in response, it was apparent she thought Lucy's status as a wallflower was already set in stone. "Revenge?" she repeated. "Hardly necessary if you're ten thousand pounds richer," she added with a grin.

"True, but what if he intends to marry me instead?"

Marianne giggled. "Oh, Lucy, I almost feel sorry for the poor sod," she replied. "See you later tonight."

Frowning, Lucy watched her friend take her leave.

Now what had her friend meant by that comment?

CHAPTER 6
AN UNCLE HELPS

*M*eanwhile, at the Foreign Office near Whitehall

For an office charged with the security of England when it came to foreign affairs, Christopher Fitzsimmons, Viscount Reardon, was always disappointed when he paid a call on his uncle. The cramped quarters meant operatives and office staff never seemed to have enough room to work.

Viscount Chamberlain's office wasn't much better, but at least he wasn't forced to share the space with others.

"Reardon?" Matthew said as he looked up from an oak desk covered with papers. If a window had been open and a breeze blew in, Christoper was sure the entire office floor would be littered with papers, for no paperweights held them in place.

"Uncle," Christopher said as he afforded the older man a nod. "Might you have a moment for me?"

Matthew stood and offered his right hand. "Of course. It's good to see you up and about. I heard you had to leave the Weatherstone's ball before it even got started last night."

"Just a case of heartburn," Christopher remarked, his fist bumping his chest. "All better now."

"Ate a bad lobster roll, didn't you?" Matthew waved him to a chair before his nephew could respond. "What's brought you here?"

"I'm looking for information—"

"Aren't we all?"

"—as to the whereabouts of my wife," Christopher said.

Matthew's brows shot up. "So you *did* marry her. Special license, I suppose?"

Christopher nodded. "It was expensive, but I thought it best we marry. Make her my viscountess before I went off to fight on the Continent. I only wish I would have moved her into Reardon Manor, no matter my mother's dislike of her."

"I'm sure Jane wanted you to marry the daughter of a duke," his uncle remarked, a bushy brow arching in dismay.

"But only an English one," Christopher replied, his expression showing his frustration. "My last letter to Maria was returned... something about the house being abandoned... and I've heard nothing from her since my return from Belgium."

Matthew displayed a grimace as he settled into his worn leather chair. "I assure you, I've heard nothing about the Conde of Albacete since his departure last May."

Christopher jerked his head back as if he'd been slapped. "You... you have someone watching him?"

Scoffing as he displayed a grimace, Matthew said, "I hardly have the funds to keep eyes on our enemies let alone on those who would be our allies. But since you had your heart set on marrying his daughter, I will admit I have been attentive should his name come up in conversation." He dipped his head. "All I ever heard was that he was desperate for a wife with some means. When he left England, he was essentially broke."

Wincing, Christopher nodded. "I knew he was in dire straights. I may have mentioned a dowry was not necessary as a means to gain his permission to marry Maria," he admitted.

This bit of news had his uncle rolling his eyes. "You're a better man than most, but I know you can afford to wed without a dowry. Did the conde witness the wedding?"

Christopher nodded. "He had to. Maria isn't yet one-and-twenty."

His uncle sighed. "The fact that you haven't heard from her is worrisome, though."

"Without a dowry, it's doubtful the conde could have married her off to someone else," Christopher remarked. "Not that she would have allowed it. She can be rather headstrong when the circumstances require it."

"Possibly," Matthew hedged, but it was apparent he didn't necessarily agree.

"Might you be willing to share where I could find John St. John? I believe he works for you, does he not?"

Giving a start, his expression conveying a combination of dismay and resignation, Matthew finally shrugged and said, "He hasn't carried documents for me since the Battle of Waterloo. Last I heard, he was back aboard his ship, so he's probably somewhere between here and Rome."

"What?"

The older viscount grinned. "Not that you should know this, but when he isn't off gathering information or delivering documents for me, he's the captain of a sailing vessel. *The Fairweather*," he stated. "Been doing it for several years."

"That's his cover?" Christopher asked in surprise.

Matthew considered how to respond. "He makes an excellent operative because he is a ship's captain," he countered. "Why is it you think *he* can be of help?"

Inhaling, Christopher let the breath out on a long sigh. "I'm fairly sure he had contact with the conde after the Battle of Waterloo," he finally said. "Someone at the hospital mentioned he had gone to Spain rather than returning to England after the war, and since his last orders involved me, I can only imagine he told the conde I'd been wounded."

Settling back into his chair, Matthew seemed to think on his answer before he said, "It's possible. If he did go to Spain, it wasn't because he had orders to do so, though." He paused as a wince crossed his face. "You do realize there were those who thought you had died that day?" he asked. "Early reports. Eye witnesses claimed you were dead before you hit the ground."

Christopher's eyes rounded as realization struck. "Do you suppose he told the conde I was dead?" He rolled his eyes. "St. John did know I was betrothed to Lady Maria, did he not?"

For a moment, it seemed as if Matthew wouldn't answer. When he finally spoke, his comment was unexpected. "So, you're sure you still wish to remain married to the Conde of Albacete's daughter?"

Christopher scoffed in disbelief. "Well, of course. I love Maria. She loves me." He stopped when Matthew held up a hand.

"All right, all right," he said on a sigh.

"Why is it you... and my mother... were so dead set against my marrying the daughter of a Spanish aristocrat?"

"It's not her," Matthew started to say. "Trust me."

"My mother's comments on the matter would suggest it *is* her."

"It's the conde," his uncle admitted. "As I said, he is broke. He never found a wife while he was in England. He needed money, so he's no doubt spent his daughter's dowry—"

"I don't need one, Uncle."

"—and yes, it is possible he's gone off and married Lady Maria to someone else."

"She left here with a copy of our marriage certificate," Christopher argued before he inhaled sharply.

"Damnation," he muttered. "I hadn't thought it possible—"

"Of course not. And if he has, at least you can take heart in knowing it wasn't her idea."

Wincing, Christopher dipped his head as if in defeat. "St. John. If he is acting as a captain—"

"He *is* a ship's captain."

"Which company employs him?"

Matthew seemed to think for a moment. "Nattersley, I believe is the name. Operates an office on the docks in Wapping."

"I'll go there now," Christopher said, rising quickly from his chair.

"Now? It will be dark soon," Matthew said. "You don't want to be in Wapping at night," he added by way of warning.

Christopher sighed. "I'll go tomorrow morning then," he replied. He paused before he added, "I appreciate your honesty, I thank you for your time. Please give my regards to Aunt Caroline and Cousin Samantha."

Matthew nodded. "I will. Do take care of yourself. We have a ball to attend tonight, and you're looking a bit peaked these days."

About to tell his uncle he would appear far healthier if he knew what had happened to his wife, Christopher decided to simply take his leave.

At least he had a clue where he could find John St. John.

CHAPTER 7
INFORMATION IS REVEALED

*M*eanwhile, on *The Fairweather*

"You're looking rather pleased with yourself," Marcus remarked when he joined Frank on the deck of *The Fairweather*. Although he had invited Sinclair and Hornsby to join them, the two had elected to stay in their cabins until *The Fairweather* was past France. The two were obviously still recovering from hangovers.

From the moment of their departure from the Thames and their entry into the Channel, a stiff breeze had filled all the sails. After the clipper passed the limestone cliffs of Dover, it joined a line of ships recently departed from Southhampton, and was soon rounding the coast of France. At their current pace, they would pass through the Strait of Gibraltar in a day or so.

Frank rested his elbows on the railing as he aimed a grin in his friend's direction. The wind ruffled his dark, sleep tousled hair, making it appear even more messy. For some reason, his dishabille didn't detract from his handsomeness. Instead, it made him seem approachable. Amiable. Friendly, even. The second son was all that and more, which had Marcus experiencing a moment of envy.

He briefly wondered what Miss Fitzsimmons thought of him.

"I am contemplating my good fortune and hoping it will hold," Frank said, loud enough to be heard over the sounds of water from beyond as the clipper sliced through the choppy waters of the Channel.

Marcus stepped back as a sudden splash of seawater threatened to drench his topcoat. "Good fortune?" he repeated. "To what do you refer?"

Frank turned and leaned against the railing so his back was to the water, his elbows bent and pressed on the wooden edge. "I took your advice and invested most of my inheritance with Mr. Grandby," he announced. "In that canal project you told me about."

Marcus' eyes rounded. "Pray tell, when was this?"

"Two days ago. It's why I was late for the Weather-stone ball," Frank replied. "As a result, I decided to secure a promise of marriage—"

"What?"

"—from Miss Marianne Harkinson. Gave her my grandmother's ring and told her we could marry after my return to England."

Marcus boggled for a moment. Never in his wildest imaginings could he envision Frank Turnbridge proposing marriage. To anyone. He was the happy-go-lucky one at school. The one with the devil-may-care attitude about his studies. The one who epitomized laziness and a lackadaisical attitude toward just about anything.

Which was probably why he was so approachable, amiable, and friendly.

"She agreed? I wasn't aware you two... have you been secretly courting her?" Marcus stammered. He had spent most of the day before contemplating how he was going to tell his best friend he was essentially betrothed, worried Frank would think him dicked in the knob.

"She agreed when I first asked her," Frank replied. "No need for courtship."

Marcus boggled. "I wasn't aware you had asked anyone to wed you."

Frank shrugged. "I was seven, I think. Decided then Marianne was the gel for me, so I haven't considered anyone else." He seemed quite pleased with himself until his eyes narrowed. "*You* weren't contemplating courting her, were you?"

Marcus held up his hands as if to ward off a blow. "No. Never," he said. "However..." He paused, deciding he had the perfect opening to tell his friend about what had happened in the gardens during the ball.

"However...?" Frank prompted.

Inhaling slowly, Marcus let out his breath in a huff and said, "I, too, have volunteered for the parson's mousetrap."

Frank stared at his friend, and continued to do so even as an arc of water splashed over the railing, dousing one of his top coat sleeves. He didn't seem to notice. "When did this happen?"

Marcus winced. "Night before last. In the gardens—"

"You were the one by the fountain?" Frank interrupted, stepping away from the railing.

Nodding, Marcus immediately realized his friend must have been somewhere nearby. "Where were you?"

"Behind the hedgerow. I would have preferred to propose with Cupid as my witness, but I feared our presence would be discovered." He moved his hands to his hips. "I wasn't aware you were courting anyone."

"I wasn't," Marcus huffed.

Frank's brows shot up. "Caught doing the deed, were you?" he teased. He suddenly sobered. "Who is the unlucky lady?"

Directing a look of annoyance at his best friend, he said, "Lucy Fitzsimmons. Reardon's sister."

Frank would have stepped back except he was already pressed against the ship's railing. "Lucy Fitzsimmons?" He let out a low whistle. "You asked her brother for his permission?"

Marcus once again winced. "In a manner of speaking." At seeing Frank's raised eyebrow as it collided with a stubborn forelock of hair, he added, "I may have asked if I might court her at one point. I meant to clarify my intentions, but I couldn't find him again at the ball—"

"He left early. Ever since he was shot by a frog on the Continent, he's been unwell. He was bedridden for months is what I hear," Frank claimed. His brows furrowed. "Who caught you?"

Scoffing, Marcus scuffed his boot on the deck. "We were only standing together by the fountain—"

"That's all it takes."

"When Lady Reardon and Lady Pettigrew—"

"It's a wonder you're alive!" Frank exclaimed as he pounded a fist against his chest. "It appears we have departed England in the nick of time." He huffed. "Too bad we won't be able to procure a copy of this week's *The Tattler*."

Marcus blinked. "What, pray tell, is *The Tattler*?"

About to answer, Frank clamped his mouth shut and glanced at the distant shores of Spain. "Just a gossip rag is all," he murmured.

A sense of panic settled over Marcus, and his heart raced at the thought of poor Miss Lucy Fitzsimmons suffering because of Lady Pettigrew.

All because he had arranged for the crone to discover them.

He hadn't considered the possibility the news of their *tête-à-tête* in the gardens would go beyond a few Mayfair parlors.

Especially not to a gossip rag.

"What makes you think anything will be printed?" he asked, managing an air of nonchalance. "Surely more newsworthy activities occurred at the ball than a mere discovery of a young couple standing together by the fountain."

Frank let out a guffaw. "*The Tattler* sells far more copies when there are such juicy scandals," he remarked.

Marcus furrowed his brows. *Poor Lucy.* "How do you know?"

Glancing first to his left and then to his right, Frank leaned toward his friend and said in a conspiratorial whisper, "I happen to know the owner and editor of the paper."

Blinking, Marcus regarded Frank with a dubious expression. "How? And who?"

"You can't tell anyone," Frank whispered, leaning in before his attention drifted to the horizon and then to a bird circling overhead. "Not even Sinclair and Hornsby," he added, glancing about for the other two young men on their way to Rome.

Marcus scoffed as he lifted his arms and waved them about. "Who am I going to tell?"

Frank rolled his eyes. "When we return, I mean. Part of the reason Felix is so good at editing that rag is because—"

"Felix?" Marcus interrupted. "Your *brother* edits *The Tattler*?" The very last person on earth he would think might be involved with any sort of newsheet was Felix Turnbridge, Earl of Fennington.

Frank nodded. "Makes a good deal of blunt from it, too, which is why I was able to wrest my inheritance from him," he explained.

"Damn," Marcus murmured. "I don't suppose I could arrange for a bribe to be paid for him to remove any mention of Lucy and me?"

Frank's expression affirmed his suspicions. The next issue was probably already printed. Probably already off the press and in the hands of the young boys who sold papers on every corner of London.

Poor Lucy!

"Gossip grows old fast," Frank said with a shrug. "After the next ball, there will no doubt be another hapless couple discovered in a state of dishabille—"

"We were not in a state of dishabille," Marcus argued.

"—fornicating in a fountain—"

"We were not *in* the fountain."

"—enjoying the scents of spring blossoms."

Marcus stared at Frank for a few seconds before his eyes widened. "*You* were fornicating in the hedgerow—"

"We were not *in* the hedgerow—"

"—and you weren't discovered."

"—because we were *behind* it. No one saw us," Frank proudly claimed.

Marcus had seen a couple hiding in the bushes, but in his haste to leave the gardens, he hadn't paused to discover their identity. He had been more concerned they might discover his, for there had been that terrible moment when he regretted everything.

Well, not *everything*.

He would never regret his kisses with Lucy. They had been wonderful. Awe-inspiring. Reason-to-live sort of moments, experienced one after the other until he was sure Lucy would agree to his marriage proposal.

Given his late father's reputation as a gambler and a debt-ridden earl, she wouldn't agree, though.

Would she?

As to why Lady Pettigrew happened to mention his drawbacks so audibly that night, he wasn't sure. *That* certainly hadn't been part of their deal. She was only supposed to discover them and threaten to spread word of their kiss. Ensure Lucy would be tied to him and only him when it came to marriage.

How else was he to ensure she would remain unbetrothed whilst he was on his Grand Tour?

The terms of her wager had been perfection. As if she knew his plan. She couldn't have known, of course. He had never professed his desire for her during their younger years playing in Hyde Park. Not like Frank had done with Marianne. He never had the courage. Once he left home for school and his father began his bouts of drinking and gambling, Marcus knew his chances of securing an agreement of marriage with any young woman would be nil.

"Not that it matters," Frank stated, bringing him out of his reverie.

"What do you mean?"

"I met with her father. The bloke gave me permission to marry Marianne even before I explained myself," he claimed. "He seemed... excited. Happy, even."

"Well, of course he did," Marcus argued. "One less thing he has to worry about when it comes to his daughter."

"I don't think that's why," Frank mused. "Said something about vexing his wife." He lifted a brow. "Anyway, he's going to give me ten thousand pounds for her dowry."

Marcus gave a start. The amount was certainly familiar. "But not until you marry," he guessed.

Frank shrugged. "True, but I'll be putting the funds into an account for Marianne and our children, so it doesn't matter."

Not having thought about a dowry, Marcus wondered if the Viscount Reardon would be bestowing one on him once he wed Lucy. Maybe after two years, Christopher Fitzsimmons would forget about why it was Lucy would be marrying him.

"Do you regret being caught?" Frank asked.

"No. But I can't help but think Lucy will hate me."

"Can't say I blame her," Frank remarked.

Marcus gave him a quelling glance. "What would you have me do?"

"You could have talked with her. Explained your plan."

"I didn't have a plan."

Frank displayed an expression of disbelief. "You knew you didn't want anyone else to have her," he accused.

Dipping his head, Marcus said, "True. But..." He allowed the sentence to trail off.

Turning to face the shores of Spain, Frank guffawed. "You, Marcus Higgins, are a coward," he announced.

Marcus allowed a grimace, knowing his friend spoke the truth.

To a point.

CHAPTER 8
TIMING IS EVERYTHING

The following morning Christopher Fitzsimmons, Viscount Reardon, regarded the offices of the Nattersley Shipping Company with an arched brow. Beneath the shingle and posted on the exterior of the wood building was a list of their vessels—all three of them—and the owner, William Nattersley.

The Fairweather, The Bellingham, and *The Arthur.*

A clerk welcomed him once he was inside, the shabby interior dark due to the dirty windows. "Are you in need of tickets, sir?"

"Information, actually. Might you know the whereabouts of John St. John? I believe he's a captain of one of your vessels? It's important I speak with him."

Nodding, the clerk turned and studied a calendar for that year. All the months were displayed in large squares. "*The Fairweather,* sir," he remarked, his quill tracing a line that ran through a series of squares representing the days of a month. "Departed yesterday morning with the tide," the clerk announced proudly. "After two stops, it should be in Rome in about a fortnight and back here..." He traced the line into the next month. "May fourth."

"Damnation," Christopher muttered.

"Did you wish to go to Rome, sir? That was *The Fairweather's* destination, but I have *The Arthur* scheduled to leave next week. It goes to Rome and then onto Athens," he offered.

"Rome?" Christopher repeated. "Pray tell, were there any passengers on board *The Fairweather*?"

"Well, of course, sir. Seven, I believe. With the wars over in France, there are a number of young men going on their Grand Tours. And couples on their wedding trips. Tradesmen."

"Marcus Higgins?" Christopher ventured. The young man had mentioned his time in London would be short. He seemed in a hurry when he had asked for a moment of his time during the Weatherstone ball.

"Yes, sir. How did you know?"

Christopher winced, momentarily annoyed for his sister's sake. "Just a lucky guess," he murmured. If he had known St. John was captaining the same ship as Higgins was scheduled to board, he would have sent the young man with a message. Surely the captain would have sent word if he knew anything about the conde or Maria.

He considered his options for a moment. "Tell me, are there any faster ships heading for Rome? Or a means to send a message to Captain St. John so it reaches one of those stops before he does? It's important."

The clerk furrowed his ginger brows. "No, sir. I don't see how. *The Bellingham* will bring back word of *The Fairweather's* location when she pulls into port, but that won't be for another fortnight."

From the various lines drawn on the calendar, Christopher realized he was truly too late. But could he wait another five weeks to speak with the captain? He almost had a thought to buy a ticket for passage to Spain, but without knowing Maria's current whereabouts, it could be months before he located her.

"I thank you for your time," he murmured.

"Of course, sir. Would you like to leave a message for the captain? For when he returns?"

Christopher considered it a moment. "If you could let him know Viscount Reardon would like a moment of his time, I would appreciate it."

The clerk's eyes widened. "Yes, my lord. Of course."

Nodding, Christopher took his leave of the shipping offices and climbed back into his town coach.

The familiar melancholy he had been experiencing since his return from the Continent settled over him.

My dearest Maria, where are you?

CHAPTER 9
MUSIC TO SOOTH THE SOUL

*L*ater that day, Worthington House in Mayfair

"I can hardly believe you're in attendance this afternoon, young lady," Lady Pettigrew said in a hoarse whisper.

Lucy stiffened in her chair before she dared a glance back to discover Mayfair's consummate gossip seated behind her. "Why good evening, Lady Pettigrew," she said sweetly. "I didn't see you come in."

The elderly matron flipped open her Oriental fan and began flicking it so quickly, Lucy thought she would create a typhoon in Lady Torrington's music salon.

"I take it you haven't read this week's issue of *The Tattler*?" the ancient matron asked in her raspy voice.

Lucy struggled to maintain a pleasant expression. Of course she had read the gossip rag. Front to back. Twice. "I do not pollute my mind with such falsities," she said quietly.

Lady Pettigrew huffed. "They are hardly falsities," she countered.

Saved from having to respond when Lady Torrington stood and welcomed them to her annual *musicale*, Lucy leaned back in her chair, determined to enjoy the evening's entertainment.

After last night's disaster of a ball—the Duke of Huntington had hosted the fête at his Mayfair mansion—Lucy had almost begged her mother to let her stay home from the Torrington *musicale*.

Jane, Viscountess Reardon, wouldn't hear of it. "It would be an admission of guilt if you don't attend," she argued. "Besides, Lord Torrington is your godfather. You're going."

So she had.

Now that she was ensconced in a high-backed chair surrounded by the creme de la creme of the aristocracy, she could almost forget what had happened the night before.

Almost.

For the first time in her life, she understood what it meant to be a wallflower. She had spent the entire evening—well, except for one dance with the zany Viscount Thistlewaite—standing on the far end of the ballroom with young ladies who Society had deemed *persona non grata*.

She might have begged her mother to take her home, except she had engaged one of the other young ladies in a discussion about ruined women. As it happened, she wasn't the only one in attendance whose exploits in the Weatherstone gardens had been detailed in *The Tattler*.

Or perhaps she was.

"I wasn't ever *in* the gardens," Lady Letitia Fetters said defensively. "Nor was Lady Louisa." Letitia appeared to be older than Lucy by at least a few years, which had her thinking the poor girl would end up a spinster.

"I was, but not in company of a member of the opposite sex," Miss Lydia Foster said as she joined them. Her ginger hair was adorned with too many decorative combs, and for a moment, Lucy wondered if she was having trouble holding up her head. An attempt had been made to hide her freckles with face powder, which had her looking so pale, she could pass as a corpse. Having been relegated to the same end of the ballroom as Lucy and Letitia, she had overheard the topic of their discussion. "My older sister escorted me so that we might see Lord Weatherstone's newest tulip, but *The Tattler* claims I was in the company of a man with the initials MH."

Letitia gave a start. "As was I!"

"Me, too," Lucy said, her brows furrowing with the realization that *The Tattler* hadn't actually printed their full names. The article had only mentioned "Miss LF."

Any one of them could have been the hapless young lady mentioned in the article.

Guilt had her swallowing, though. Three other young women with the initials "LF" had suffered for her transgression.

"Why, I do believe we're all speaking of the same

article," she said in a quiet voice. The two girls exchanged quick glances. "Page six?" she added.

They nodded as their gloved hands went to cover their open mouths.

"It wasn't about me or Louisa," Letitia murmured.

"Nor me," Lydia said, her eyes rounding in understanding.

When the two directed their attentions solely on Lucy, she couldn't help the heat that had her face turning a bright pink. "Oh, dear," she said, angling her head to one side. "Who could this mysterious Miss LF and MH be?" she asked innocently.

Both girls fisted their gloved hands to their waists and huffed their obvious displeasure with her. A moment later, and she was all alone. Well, alone if one didn't consider the potted palm she had been using to hide behind most of the night.

At least Marianne had joined her on occasion—when she hadn't been happily dancing with every young buck in attendance.

She could do that now that she had her future husband sorted. She no longer had to censure her words to suit a male's easily bruised ego. She could speak on topics other than the weather and the number of dancers in attendance. She could attend entertainments without a care as to who hosted them or in whose company she would be seen.

Marianne had become the young woman Lucy wished to be.

Unfettered. Carefree. Happy.

. . .

*L*ucy was pulled from her reverie when their hostess completed her welcoming statements and introduced her husband.

Milton Grandby, Earl of Torrington, joined his fairly new wife, Adele, in front of the assemblage and kissed her on the cheek, which had most in attendance tittering behind their gloves and Adele displaying a blush of embarrassment. "I can't help myself," he said, directing his comment to the audience. "I adore this woman. Always have. Do enjoy the performance." And then, as if he didn't think anyone would hear, he added, "They certainly cost enough," in a hoarse whisper.

A chorus of titters and gasps sounded in response, helping to drown out Adele's scolding, "Milton!"

Grinning behind her gloved hand, Lucy felt elation. Her godfather had always been able to make people feel welcome. He had always been able to put people at ease. To make them laugh when they probably shouldn't. To remind them things weren't as bad as they seemed.

He had been two years younger than Lucy when he inherited the Torrington earldom, eschewing marriage until he was well into his forties.

All because he wanted Adele Slater Worthington to be his wife. Given her marriage to an early steamship magnate, he had been forced to wait until she was widowed to begin paying calls on her. After an entire Season spent in one another's company at every *ton* event, they married.

Lucy thought briefly of Frank Turnbridge. He wanted Marianne as his wife and had done what he needed to do to ensure their future. Now Marianne was happy as a lark.

The music from three stringed instruments quieted those in the parlor, the selection a pleasing piece by a German composer. Although she wasn't aware of it initially, the rhythm seemed to match her experience of the past few days. The excitement of being asked by Marcus to join her in the gardens. The pause when she had proposed the wager. The awe she had felt during their series of kisses. The shock of realizing what they had done. The fear at being discovered. The disgust when she realized Marcus had taken his leave. The sorrow of learning she would now be considered a ruined woman.

As the composition crescendoed to its end, Lucy experienced a revelation that had her gaze darting in the direction of Marianne.

What if Marcus had done the same as Frank? Secured a promise of her hand in marriage, only in a more clumsy fashion?

She had to stifle the scoff that threatened to erupt from her throat. She hadn't even met Marcus Higgins prior to the Weatherstone ball.

Had she?

She once again glanced over at Marianne, whose attention was on the musicians, her expression as pleasant as her appearance. As if she sensed Lucy's gaze, she glanced at her and raised an eyebrow.

Lucy mouthed, "Find me later."

Marianne's frown indicated she didn't understand.

Not about to draw any attention to herself, Lucy settled back in her chair and directed her gaze on the musicians.

Had she met Marcus when they were younger?

Perhaps they had known one another when they were children, playing in Hyde Park under the watchful eyes of their nurses. Unlike Marianne, she couldn't recall any marriage proposals by the boys with whom she and Marianne had played, but at that age, she would have laughed it off.

Another glance in Marianne's direction had her furrowing her brows. Her best friend appeared happy. Relaxed. Satisfied.

And why shouldn't she?

Marianne knew her future.

Didn't Lucy know her own as well?

She blinked at the realization that either Marcus would marry her or he would pay her ten thousand pounds. Either way, her future was set.

Even if she had to play the part of a wallflower for the next two years, she knew what her future held.

Marriage to Marcus Higgins or life as a well-to-do spinster with her own bank account.

Christopher would have to see to the account, of course, but she wouldn't have to rely on her brother for her living. As such, Lucy realized she could behave exactly like Marianne was doing.

She was essentially betrothed, even if Marcus

Higgins intended to pay her what he owed her instead of marrying her.

By the time the *musicale* ended, Lucy was displaying a beatific smile and feeling ever so satisfied.

Wallflowerhood might be more tolerable than she had imagined. She would have her revenge on London's society, and her revenge on Lady Pettigrew, if the hag lived that long.

CHAPTER 10
MUSINGS ON A GLOOMY DAY

*M*eanwhile, on board *The Fairweather*

"She should have received my letter by now," Marcus murmured, his gaze on the gray waterline beyond the porthole window in their cabin. He had his elbows resting in the frame, the wood's varnish having worn off long ago.

"What's this?" Frank looked up from the book he was reading, his lanky body stretched out on the top bunk so his feet stuck out beyond the end of the bed.

"Lucy. I wondered if she's received my letter," Marcus said, pushing away from the window. With that day's sheets of rain and gloomy gray skies, the two hadn't taken their usual walkabout on the deck after breakfast. At least the wind wasn't blowing too much with the storm, but it meant the rain had continued well into the afternoon.

"You honestly think that hapless porter in Wapping was going to see to its delivery?" Frank asked as he closed his book. He thrust his legs out over the edge of the bunk and jumped down. "He's probably already spent the coin you tossed him."

"I'm sure he passed it along to someone who could see to its delivery," Marcus argued. "He seemed... determined," he added, remembering how the young man had gone out of his way to capture the folded document. Although his father had developed a doubt about anyone and everyone in London—the Foreign Office's investigation involving him in a gambling scheme had cost him his reputation, even if it hadn't been responsible for draining his bank account— Marcus still had faith in those who took coins to run errands. If he couldn't trust the caddies and street urchins in London, he didn't think he could trust anyone.

"Say it was delivered," Frank said as he placed the book on the cabin's only table and sat in one of the chairs. "Who ended up with it?"

"Well, Lucy, of course. It had her name on it."

Frank gave him a quelling glance. "For someone who has two sisters, I thought you would know that no missives get delivered to the girls in a household unless they're secreted in by way of their lady's maids. Or footmen who can be bribed."

Marcus blinked. "I didn't know that." His eyes rounded. "If it doesn't get delivered to Lucy, then who...?" He clamped his mouth shut and made a sound of disgust in the back of his throat.

"Her older brother, of course," Frank said as he pulled

a deck of cards from his pocket. "Or mayhap her mother, if Reardon is still feeling under the weather."

"What's this?" Marcus joined Frank at the table as his friend shuffled the cards. He dared a glance at the book before lifting it to read the gold foil-stamped title, *A Traveller's Guide to Greece*.

"What's what?"

"Why is Lord Reardon feeling under the weather?"

Dealing the cards, Frank lifted a shoulder. "Felix said he got shot when he was in one of the battles last year, but he's kept the severity of it from the family. Didn't want the women worrying about him," he explained. "He was at the ball the other night but left after a half-hour. Complained of heartburn."

"Must have had one of the lobster rolls," Marcus murmured, picking up his cards to order them by number.

Frank scoffed as he arranged his cards. "Only champagne. He frequently suffers from the malady, if I'm to believe my brother."

Marcus glanced up from his cards and furrowed a brow. "From his being shot, do you suppose?"

Frank set out a pair of cards. "Don't think so. Probably due to his mother. Or Lady Pettigrew."

Fumbling his play, Marcus was quick to recapture his cards before Frank could see them. "What do you mean?"

Leaning back in his chair, Frank said, "If I had Lady Reardon as my mother and that gossip Pettigrew in my house, I would have constant heartburn, too."

"Pettigrew's a... a *gossip*?"

Frank blinked in disbelief before a chuckle erupted. "A consummate gossip. The worst. Or the best, if you can believe my brother. She supplies information to him for *The Tattler*."

The cards in Marcus' hands dropped to the table. "What?"

Furrowing his brows, Frank said, "Surely you knew."

Panic had Marcus rising from the chair so quickly, it fell backward and would have fallen to the floor except the wall was close enough to catch it. "Dammit," he cursed under his breath.

"What is it?"

"I trusted her," he said, planting his hands on either side of the porthole window. Despite the rain having stopped, the gray beyond seemed darker than before.

"You trusted Lady Pettigrew?" Frank asked, his cards forgotten. "With... with what?"

Marcus threw up his hands and displayed a wince. "I arranged for her to... to come into the gardens. To find Lucy and me."

"What?" Now it was Frank's turn to quickly rise from his chair. It fell backwards, hitting the wooden planks with a resounding *thud*. "You *wanted* to be caught?" he asked in disbelief.

Nodding, Marcus laced his fingers behind his head and stalked back and forth in front of the window. "It seemed like a good idea at the time," he murmured. "But I didn't want the entire *ton* to know about us."

One of his dark brows furrowing in confusion, Frank seemed to think on his friend's response before his face brightened in understanding. "You really are sweet on Lucy Fitzsimmons," he whispered.

Marcus sighed. "I am. Have been ever since I first met her."

"At the ball?" Frank guessed. "I've heard of love at first sight, but—"

"No. Not at the ball. When we were... younger." He huffed. "Like you and your Marianne," he added.

The mention of Marianne had Frank grinning. "I like the sound of that. 'Your Marianne'."

"Well, obviously, if you've gone and given her a ring and a promise of marriage," Marcus reasoned.

"Is that what you wanted from Lucy? A promise of marriage?"

Marcus nodded. "Something like that. Wasn't hard to get, either, although..." He paused and shrugged. "She's probably expecting ten thousand pounds."

Frank rocked back on his heels, which wasn't hard when the ship suddenly rolled slightly from a wave. "Why would she be expecting ten thousand pounds?"

When the ship rolled again, Marcus retook the chair. "She... she made a wager. Said if we were caught or if I told anyone what we'd done, I would either have to marry her or pay her ten thousand pounds."

Frank's whistle filled the small cabin. "You don't have ten thousand pounds."

"Do tell," Marcus responded.

"But you wanted to get caught."

Marcus nodded. "In her company. Not necessarily... not in a compromising position," he stammered. "I only meant for there to be a sort of promise of our eventual betrothal. I had no time for courtship. I haven't been in London since I left for school, and I feared if I didn't do something drastic, I would lose the chance with her."

"So you did what I did," Frank accused.

Shaking his head, Marcus scoffed. "You and Marianne... you've known your whole life you two would wed."

"Well, not exactly," he started to argue. "But I see your point."

"I only knew I couldn't bear the thought of Lucy Fitzsimmons with someone else."

Frank furrowed a brow. "Pardon my confusion, but did she even remember you? *Does* she remember you?"

Marcus inhaled to answer before dipping his head. "I don't think so. At least, if she did, she didn't let on." His gaze once again darted to the window. "I can't say I blame her. I've been gone from London since I was ten years old."

Frank suppressed a yawn and lifted his chair from the floor. "How did you two know one another?"

Leaning back, Marcus said, "Same way as you know Marianne. From our time playing in Hyde Park. She and Marianne..." He shrugged. "Well, as I recall, you declared your love for Marianne when we were, what? Four years old?" he guessed.

"Six," Frank corrected him, his manner suggesting he was quite proud of the fact. "She was three at the time."

Chuckling, Marcus rolled his eyes. "I don't recall that

far back," he murmured. "But I remember our nurses… their group grew larger the older we got."

"Strength in numbers," Frank said. "Safety, too."

"The number of children grew, as well."

"Well, it wasn't as if our parents stopped fornicating after we were born," Frank murmured.

Marcus displayed a grimace. Although Frank didn't have younger brothers or sisters, Marcus' mother died giving birth to his younger sister, Beatrice.

"The gels started forming their own groups and us boys were left to fend for ourselves."

Marcus nodded. "That, I remember." He winced. "That was when I noticed Lucy. She was like a shining beacon in the middle of all those giggly girls."

"As I recall, she was their leader," Frank whispered.

"Oldest girl in the family. I remember looking her up in one of those peerage books."

"A Fitzsimmons, is she not?"

Sighing, Marcus nodded. "Her father did something heroic over on the Continent and was afforded a viscountcy. I never thought I'd hear the end of it from my father."

"What are you saying?"

"A viscountcy," Marcus repeated. "Most war heroes are lucky to get a knighthood. Father claimed Lord Chamberlain must have used his influence as head of the Foreign Office to encourage the king to bestow his younger brother, Christopher, with the title. Now his son, also named Christopher, has the title."

"And a bullet wound," Frank reminded him.

"Lucy is Lord Chamberlain's niece."

Frank stared at him, his expression blank.

"I never told my father I wanted to court Lucy. I would have been disowned, you see," Marcus claimed.

Shifting uncomfortably in his chair, Frank cursed softly. "What about your brother, Max? Have you told him?" Everyone in the *ton* knew that since Maxwell Higgins finally met his Maker, his newly-married oldest son, Max, was left mired in debt. Max was already running the earldom as best he could from the country estate in Staffordshire, his bitterness towards his father well known. Rumors suggested he planned to marry an aristocrat's daughter, no doubt to secure her dowry.

Marcus shook his head. "I haven't told him. I haven't told anyone except you." He hadn't even told Lucy. "So imagine my surprise when Lucy suggested the wager. No matter what happened, I would gain her hand in marriage if someone learned of our time in the Weather-stone gardens."

Frank whistled softly. "And then Lady Pettigrew appeared."

Once again wincing, Marcus settled into his chair. "She probably hates me."

"Oh, I rather think Lady Pettigrew is happy as a lark," Frank countered.

"I was speaking of Lucy, you idiot."

The way Frank grinned, Marcus realized he knew what he meant.

"Chin up, Higgins," Frank said as he leaned back. "In

two years, we'll return to British shores to claim our ladies, and it will be as if none of this had happened."

Marcus regarded his friend with a wan grin. "I can only hope you're right, but I rather doubt it," he murmured.

He was almost glad when Sinclair and Hornsby joined them for the game of cards.

CHAPTER 11
A MISSIVE ARRIVES

eanwhile, at Reardon Manor

"I apologize for disturbing you, my lord, but a letter has been delivered."

Christopher, Viscount Reardon, looked up from a ledger spread open on the desk in his study and glanced at the servant. "Add it to the pile," he murmured, gesturing to the salver Peters had brought him after the morning post had arrived.

The silver salver was littered with a number of invitations and missives Christopher knew were invoices.

The beginning of the Season always brought with it the bills for modistes and tailors, shoemakers and milliners. Allowing his mother to keep up with the latest fashions had meant he could claim he couldn't afford to court a future Viscountess Reardon whenever his mother brought up the topic of him marrying.

Keeping Maria a secret from her had him feeling both guilt and giddiness. He wasn't sure how he was going to break the news to her that he was already a married man.

Despite having inherited the viscountcy the year prior, he had spent more time recovering from his wound than overseeing his lands. His words to his uncle about forgoing a dowry when it came to Maria hadn't been entirely truthful. Until he could meet with his man of business, he had no idea how much he could spend on a wife.

Peters approached the desk but paused with the folded note still clutched in his hand.

Christopher glanced up. "What is it?"

"It was delivered by a street urchin, sir, and it is addressed to Miss Fitzsimmons."

Leaning back in his chair, Christopher regarded the missive as if it might explode. "A street urchin?" he repeated. Intrigued, he took the note from the butler and studied the masculine scrawl on one side. The ink had been smudged, and the once-white parchment appeared as if it had been stepped on, doused in water, and nibbled on one edge. "So it is," Christopher whispered.

Normally, he would give such a note to his mother. Let her read any correspondence addressed to his sister and let her decide if it was safe to pass along to Lucy.

This one had him curious, though.

He gave the butler a dismissive nod and began undoing the tight envelope in which the note had been folded. After a struggle, he finally had the parchment spread out and mostly flattened on his desk.

Dear Miss Fitzsimmons,

I owe you an apology for what happened last night, although I must admit, I am not sorry for having kissed you. I found the experience most illuminating, for it opened my eyes to the possibility of what is to come in my life. Of what I may look forward to for the rest of my life.

I do hope you are able to see it the same.

Here Christopher blinked several times before a snort erupted. So Lucy *had* been kissing Marcus Higgins in the gardens! She had as much as admitted to liking it, too. Despite the seriousness of the situation, he couldn't help the grin that split his face.

He continued reading.

As per our agreement, I will of course marry you. I look forward to the day when we will say our vows and take up residence in Pendleton House in Mayfair.

"Damnation," Christopher muttered softly, his grin slowly fading as he contemplated what sort of agreement his sister may have made. They had talked about her wager, but marriage hadn't been mentioned. Ten thousand pounds had been, though.

Marcus had asked his permission to court her. During the Weatherstone ball. In that moment, Christopher had been suffering too much to realize to what he was agreeing. The young man had been so earnest, though.

Christopher was about to send for Lucy when he remembered she was with their mother at Lady Torrington's *musicale*.

He resumed reading, settling back into his chair while he held the wrinkled parchment between both hands.

> *There is a slight matter of timing, however. I have only this morning boarded a sailing vessel bound for Rome as I have embarked on my Grand Tour. Frank Turnbridge and I made the arrangements well before our terms at Cambridge ended last week. The itinerary will keep us away from British shores for two years.*

Christopher sighed at the reminder of what he had learned that morning at the shipping company offices. This letter from Marcus confirmed what the clerk had told him. He could only imagine how Lucy would react to this bit of information. Either she would be spitting mad or she would be relieved.

For a moment, he once again wondered what *he* should think of his sister married to Marcus Higgins. Other than the few minutes he had spent in the young man's company at the ball—Marcus had asked if he might speak with him on an important matter and then blurted the reason before Christopher could respond— he was barely acquainted with him, and that had been when he was a child.

Marcus had been one of the children with whom he and others who lived in Park Lane and South Audley

Street played in Hyde Park. That was long before Marcus' father, the Earl of Greenley, had gained a reputation as a gambler. Before he was said to be deep in debt.

Christopher dropped the letter to his desk.

How could Marcus Higgins afford his Grand Tour? From where had he secured the funds?

Filing away the questions for later perusal, he retrieved the letter and resumed reading.

> *Upon my return, I shall pay a call to renew our acquaintance so that a date can be set for our wedding. I do hope this will not inconvenience you. It will give you two years to attend the entertainments of the ton with the knowledge you no longer need to impress a young man into proposing marriage.*
>
> *Let this letter be a formal acknowledgment of our betrothal. Upon my return to British shores, I will pay a call to seek your brother's formal permission to marry you.*
>
> *Please know that I shall think about you often as I visit Ancient Greek temples, for I know it was Cupid who was responsible for our meeting again, and every statue of Aphrodite will have me dreaming of you.*
>
> *Yours in service,*
> *Marcus Higgins*

"Meeting again?" Christopher said aloud. He reread the name several times in an effort to decipher the writing, finally affirming it was indeed the younger Greenley whelp. "Damnation."

He set aside the letter and leaned back in his chair. Of all the possible news he expected could be found in a letter to his sister, this was the most *unexpected*.

Marcus Higgins, second son of the Earl of Greenley, was apparently more serious about marrying his sister than he had supposed from their brief meeting at the Weatherstone ball. And apparently they had some sort of an agreement to that end.

Christopher could think of a dozen reasons why he should be happy for his sister. Someone she apparently wanted to marry had agreed to her terms—he would have to find out whatever *those* were—and the young man would return for her after his Grand Tour was complete.

Their mother would no longer have to be concerned about who Lucy would marry. In two more years, Lucy would be out of Reardon Manor and be the lady of Pendleton House.

The reminder that Marcus Higgins was the son of the Earl of Greenley had Christopher wincing once again. Everyone knew the late earl had been a gambler. Apparently in debt up to his eyeballs when he died.

How did Marcus intend to keep a wife, if not with her dowry? Their brief discussion at the Weatherstone ball hadn't delved into such details. And how did the young man intend to tell his brother he was going to marry the niece of his nemesis? Everyone knew the Earl of Greenley had hated Viscount Chamberlain even if it made no sense.

Glad he hadn't allowed his mother to read the

missive, Christopher quickly refolded it and stuffed it into his waistcoat pocket.

At the sound of Peters greeting his mother and sister, he straightened in his chair and returned his attention to the ledger. As he expected, they both paused outside the study to greet him.

"How was the *musicale*?" he asked, feigning interest. Although he, too, had received an invitation, he had opted to remain at Reardon Manor. Attending the fête would have had Lady Reardon attempting to match him to some hapless young lady in need of a husband.

"It was truly *wonderful*," Lucy said brightly. "I am so glad I went. It's always good to see my godfather."

From the expression on his mother's face, Christopher had a thought his sister was lying. "I'm relieved to hear it. I take it Lady Pettigrew wasn't in attendance?"

"Oh, but she was," Lucy replied, her pleasant expression unwavering. "Oh, and Lady Marianne asked after you. She was quite worried. I told her you were up and about."

"Thank you," he responded. "I shall have to thank her for her concern at the next ball. And you, Mother?"

Jane clutched her reticule to her lilac-garbed chest as if she expected someone to rob her. "I had a very pleasant time. And you? Are you feeling better?"

"Right as rain," he replied. "I'll see you at dinner."

"Of course, darling."

Christopher cleared his throat. "Oh, Lucy, might you remain a moment? I have something to ask you if you're not otherwise engaged?"

The two women exchanged curious glances, but their mother merely lifted a shoulder and headed for the stairs.

"What is it?" Lucy asked as she made her way into the study. The sound of her footsteps was swallowed up by the Turkish carpet, its wool worn where her late father had paced when he was worried.

"Close the door," Christopher said quietly.

Her eyes widening in surprise, Lucy was quick to do his bidding. "What's this about?" she asked in a whisper.

Christopher pulled the missive from his pocket and held it up by one corner. "I understand best wishes are in order."

Reaching out to take the note, Lucy said, "Best wishes for whom?"

He pulled the note away from her fingers before she could grasp it, his brows furrowing with suspicion.

Lucy gasped. "How did you find out about Lady Marianne?" she asked in surprise.

Christopher's brows shot up nearly as high as his hairline. "Lady Marianne is betrothed?"

About to respond in the positive, Lucy's gaze darted to the note and then back to her brother. "You can't say a word to anyone. Her mother doesn't know. Her father knows, but he wants to keep it a secret from his wife," she blurted. "Apparently he likes to vex her."

He seemed to think on her response a moment before he indicated the chair in front of his desk. "Have a seat, Sister."

"You won't tell?"

A grimace appeared on his face. "Lady Marianne's secret is safe with me," he assured her. "Yours, however, is not."

Lucy gave a start. "What are you talking about?"

He once again held up the note. "This came today. For you," he stated. He tossed it across the desk, and Lucy caught it in both hands. She glanced down at the address and furrowed her brows.

"It certainly appears as if it's traveled a good distance," she remarked. "May I open it?"

Nodding, Christopher dared a glance out the window behind his desk and sighed as Lucy peeled apart the corners of the parchment. From the way she used only her fingertips, it was apparent she thought the missive contained bad news.

"It's from Marcus Higgins," Christopher stated. "You will tell me now of your agreement with him."

Lucy gasped, her eyes darting over the scrawl filling the page. "I'm not sure I can make out what any of this says," she murmured in frustration. "His penmanship is appalling."

"He has agreed to marry you," Christopher stated without preamble. "Which has me wondering. Did you *propose* to him?"

Blinking several times, Lucy shook her head. "No!" She blinked again. "Well, not exactly."

Christopher crossed his arms and lifted a brow in response.

"I told you. We made a wager. Remember?"

"A wager that he would pay you ten thousand pounds if you were discovered," Christopher responded.

She nodded.

"So... what's this about him agreeing to marry you?"

"*What?*" Lucy swallowed, her attention once again returning to the letter. Once she had decoded Marcus' messy script, she was able to read most of the missive. "If he didn't pay me the ten thousand pounds, he had to marry me," she murmured, her attention still on the letter.

"So... you got him to agree to either pay you or marry you?" Christopher asked in disbelief. He chuckled softly, remembering how nervous Marcus had been at the ball. How tongue-tied he had been when he had asked permission to court Lucy. How relieved Marcus had seemed when he had given his blessing.

It wasn't until he was on his way home, in a great deal of pain, when it dawned on him that Marcus might not have a penny to his name.

Christopher was pulled from his reverie when he noticed Lucy absently nodding. "If they allowed women at White's, I'd take you there to make *my* wagers," he murmured.

Glancing up from the letter, Lucy said, "Again? What does he mean by that?"

Christopher arched a single brow. "I wondered about that, too. At first."

Exhaling softly, Lucy seemed confused. "I wasn't aware we had already met," she whispered as if to herself.

"You obviously made an impression on him at some point in your life. At a ball, perhaps?"

She shook her head. "He hasn't been in London since he left for school," she remembered him saying. "When he was ten, I think," she added quietly.

"So... you played with him in Hyde Park. With all the rest of the brats from Park Lane and South Audley Street," he reasoned.

"You were one of those brats once," she accused, but her unfocussed gaze suggested she was attempting to remember everyone she had ever played with in the park.

"I was," he admitted. "As I recall, he was there. With the Turnbridge boys. The Combers. All the Harrington children." He rolled his eyes. "Every nurse brought at least two whelps, and there were a dozen of us at any one time."

Lucy allowed a wan grin. "I remember," she said, although it was apparent she didn't specifically recall Marcus.

Christopher stood and reached across the desk to chuck her chin. "Marry him," he said. "He might be poor, but you'll have your dowry to live on, and he can provide protection."

Her eyes widening in shock, Lucy gave her head a shake. "But... I'd rather have the ten thousand pounds," she argued.

He chuckled. "Wouldn't we all?" He leaned back and retook his chair.

"Aren't you offended he didn't ask your permission?" she countered.

Shaking his head, Christopher said, "But he did. In a manner of speaking," he hedged, allowing a soft chuckle upon remembering how nervous the young man seemed that night. And why not? His request for a moment of Christopher's time was quickly followed by the reason he wanted said time, the words tumbling out so quickly, Marcus had asked permission to court Lucy before he'd had a chance to propose a meeting.

"Before the dancing at the Weatherstone ball had even begun," Christopher murmured, emerging from his reverie with a grin on his face. He had a hard time suppressing more humor at seeing his sister's reaction to his claim. "Timed his request perfectly, given I had to take my leave not ten minutes later," he added as a hand went to his chest.

"Because you gave him permission," she accused, scoffing at realizing this was all her brother's fault.

He chuckled. "I could blame it on a bad lobster roll," he insisted. Frowning at seeing her look of dismay, he added, "No matter what, nothing will happen for two years. He's off on his Grand Tour."

About to remind him she would still be a wallflower, Lucy remembered what she had decided at the *musicale*.

Her future was set.

According to Marcus and now her brother, she was betrothed.

Ruined or not, she was betrothed.

Apparently Christopher noticed the change in her, for he swallowed. Hard.

"Then I do hope Mr. Higgins is prepared for my

response when he returns to England," she stated, lifting her chin in defiance.

"Lucy," Christopher said in a voice filled with warning.

"Oh. Don't you 'Lucy' me," she replied, standing up so quickly, the chair in which she'd been seated threatened to fall backward. "I intended to take my revenge upon London society and Lady Pettigrew by *enjoying* my time as a wallflower. With ten thousand pounds in my future, I could have been independent. A well-to-do spinster—"

"Would not have happened, Lucy," her brother interrupted, rolling his eyes.

"Now I'll have to take my revenge on Marcus Higgins. If he thinks—"

"Lucy!"

She recoiled in surprise at hearing how loudly Christopher said her name. Had they been children, their nurse would have scolded him. "What?" she managed in a small voice.

"He's a good man. Do not hold the sins of his father against him," he said in a near whisper.

Lucy displayed a look of confusion. "This isn't about the Earl of Greenley," she said with a scoff. "This is about his second son, agreeing to a wager—"

"For which *you* set the terms and which you have clearly won," Christopher finished for her. "Congratulations."

Apparently appeased by his acknowledgment, Lucy

took a deep breath and let it out. "Thank you," she said in a whisper. "If there's nothing else...?"

"Consider yourself betrothed, Sister," he interrupted. "I'll check with our man of business as to your dowry to ensure that you and the children will be taken care of."

"I appreciate your concern."

Christopher furrowed a brow. "Do not discount his intentions," he warned.

Lucy recoiled at hearing his tone of voice. He had clearly sided with Marcus Higgins. "Why not?"

"I think he loves you," he said in a quiet voice.

From Lucy's reaction, he knew she hadn't considered Marcus' regard for her.

"If he loved me, he wouldn't have left me," she countered with a huff.

"He loved you enough to secure your hand in marriage before leaving England," Christopher countered. "To be sure you wouldn't go off and marry someone else. Apparently much like Frank Turnbridge did with Lady Marianne."

Lucy's hands went to her hips, the letter scrunched in one fist. "He never actually *proposed* marriage." She held up her right hand. "Nor did he give me a ring."

Christopher chuckled softly. "He didn't have to propose," he said in a whisper. "Since you did so with your wager."

From the way Lucy dipped her head, Christopher knew he had struck a nerve. She might be stubborn and she might be proud, but she was also coming to realize she had fallen into a trap she had set herself.

He watched as she, once again huffing softly, moved to the door. "You do realize I have been relegated to the life of a wallflower until he makes good on the wager?"

Blinking twice, Christopher considered how to respond. No matter what he said, he knew she would be angry with him, perhaps for a very long time. "You? A wallflower?" He shook his head. "I rather imagine there will be a bevy of young ladies striving to become wallflowers so they might bask in your wallflower glow."

Lucy rolled her eyes and took her leave of the study, slamming the door shut behind her.

Settling back into his chair, Christopher clasped his hands together at the back of head and grinned broadly.

He could hardly wait until Marcus Higgins returned to British shores.

He could only hope the hapless young man wouldn't change his mind in the meantime.

Taking up a sheet of stationery, Christoper penned a short letter to Max Higgins, Earl of Greenley, apprising him that his younger brother had made arrangements to marry Lucy upon his return to British shores. Although he mentioned a hope that the late earl's dislike of their uncle wouldn't result in a family rift, his main reason for writing was one of curiosity.

Has Marcus been the beneficiary of some distant relative's fortune? And if not, how was it he could go on his Grand Tour and accept a wager worth ten thousand pounds?

I ask only out of concern for my sister, Lucy, as she is now betrothed to him.

I look forward to your earliest reply.

Sincerely yours,

Christopher Fitzsimmons

Rt. Hon Viscount Reardon

CHAPTER 12
A CAPTAIN OFFERS A PLAN

*M*eanwhile, on *The Fairweather*

"Are you awake?"

Marcus' voice had Frank waking with a start. "What's that?"

"Oh, good. You're awake."

Frank groaned. "Because you woke me up," he accused. "Do you have any idea what was about to happen to me?" he asked rhetorically.

Wincing, Marcus said, "You were about to win a game of whist?" he guessed.

He could hear the disbelief in his best friend's voice when Frank said, "Marianne was about to kiss my prick, which is hard as a rock and ready for whatever else she was going to let me do to her."

Marcus sighed. "Sorry."

There was a moment of silence before Frank said, "Well? Why did you wake me?"

"I was thinking..."

A groan sounded from above before Frank's face appeared from over the edge of the upper bunk. "No thinking. We're on our Grand Tour. We've been planning this for—"

"I know, I know," Marcus said. "I just... I was thinking I might go back to England earlier than we discussed."

"You are not going back to England," Frank insisted. "We have made arrangements. We have reservations. We are going to see all the Ancient Greek and Roman sites. We are going to eat unusual foods and drink wines we've only dreamt of. We might even bed a woman or two," he added, his hands flying about to punctuate his points.

"We are?"

Frank groaned in frustration. "Someone has to show us what to do when we bed our wives," he reasoned. "The best way, I mean. I rather doubt that serving wench at The Old Anchor was the best instructor."

Marcus wasn't about to mention he had never been with the older woman Frank mentioned. At least, not in that way. "Agreed," he hedged. "But... I didn't actually propose marriage to Miss Fitzsimmons."

Frank frowned and pulled his elbow beneath him so he could once again lean over the edge of the bunk. "What were you doing with her in the gardens, if not proposing marriage? I thought... I thought that was the plan."

"It was," Marcus assured him. "But she brought up the wager and... I accepted the terms."

"Which means you're betrothed," Frank stated,

shrugging. He settled back onto his bunk, tossing the blanket off the edge.

Marcus cleared his throat, which had Frank allowing an audible sigh. There was a moment of silence before Marcus said, "What if she will only accept the money? Instead of marriage?"

Frank's sound of disbelief was loud in the darkness. "I rather doubt Lucy Fitzsimmons plans to be a spinster," he reasoned. "If Lady Pettigrew discovered you in the gardens, you've been featured in *The Tattler* and all of Mayfair has heard the tale. She's ruined, I tell you. At best, she'll be a wallflower—"

"That's exactly *why* I need to go back," Marcus interrupted. "She no doubt hates me. If I wait two years, she'll despise me so intensely, I shall never gain her good graces, and then I really will owe her ten thousand pounds and gain nothing in return when I'm finally able to pay her."

The cabin was silent for so long, Marcus thought Frank might have dozed off. If he had, he couldn't blame his best friend. They had been aboard ship only a few days and already he was becoming the least likable travel companion—all because of his bungled marriage proposal.

Turning onto his side, he closed his eyes and was about to succumb to sleep when Frank said, "I think we're going through the Strait of Gibraltar."

Marcus opened his eyes and listened intently. The faint sounds of whoops and hollers came from somewhere above them. "Should we go up?" he asked.

"Let's," Frank said, his legs already dangling over the edge of his bunk. "It will be two more years before we see it again."

Sighing, Marcus donned his banyan and followed Frank out the cabin door and up the companionway. Apparently the ruckus had roused Sinclair and Hornsby as well, for the two followed them to the deck. At the top of the stairs, the four stared in wonder, Frank's attention on Point Marroquí to the north and Marcus' gaze on Point Cires to the south. Hornsby rushed to the starboard railing while Sinclair moved to the port railing. A nearly full moon illuminated the clouds from behind, casting the top of the water in a dull gray.

"What's all the racket?" Marcus asked in a whisper, turning to find Frank heading to the railing.

"Monkeys," Frank murmured. He gave a start when a loud splash occurred not far off the bow.

"What was that?" Sinclair asked, stepping back from the railing.

"Whale's tail," Marcus said in awe, his attention on where the water had swallowed up the evidence of the large mammal.

"Are those dolphins?" Frank asked, his arm reaching out as a means of showing where his gaze was directed.

"They are indeed," Captain St. John replied from behind them. He had just come out of the wheelhouse. "I apologize if my men woke you," he added as he joined them at the railing. "Rodney, my first mate, has orders to alert the crew when we come through the strait."

"I wouldn't have wanted to miss this," Hornsby

replied, pulling his banyan tighter around his middle. Given the breeze, the spring night was chilly.

"What are those lights on the water?" Frank asked.

"Other ships," Captain St. John replied. "The strait is a bottleneck of sorts. It's not quite eight miles wide at its narrowest, and lots of ships go through here day and night. I like to have one of my crew in the crow's nest to be on the lookout for ships, just in case one gets too close."

The five continued to lean against the railing until St. John yawned and said, "I'm going back to bed. See you all at breakfast."

"Good night, Captain," the young men murmured in unison. About to settle back against the railing, Marcus added, "Oh, Captain?"

St. John paused at the door to his cabin. "Yes?"

"Will the ship be stopping at any ports before it reaches Rome?"

The captain chuckled. "Are you already looking to get off?" He rejoined them at the railing.

"No... I just wondered if I might be able to send a letter, is all," Marcus said, well aware of how Frank rolled his eyes. The other two wandered off in the direction of the companionway, their wide yawns accompanied by comments about returning to their beds.

"Ah, you've left behind a gel, have you?" the captain teased.

"Something like that," Marcus admitted sheepishly.

"Did she see you off from London?"

Marcus dipped his head. "Uh, no. I sent her a note, though. I didn't really have a chance to explain—"

"What's this?" St. John interrupted, quickly sobering.

"I didn't tell her I was leaving when I saw to it... well, that we'd... well..."

"Spit it out, young man," St. John insisted. "I can't be telling you what to do if you don't give me all the details."

Frank groaned. "I've heard all this," he said. "I'm going back to bed."

The captain watched Frank's departure before he turned his attention back on Marcus. "Start from the beginning, and if you have me yawning even once, I'm going to request we take it up again at breakfast."

Marcus blinked. "All right. I think I have loved Miss Lucy Fitzsimmons since I was rather young. I decided I wanted to secure a promise of marriage before I left on this trip, so I..." He paused, his face screwing up into a grimace.

"Go on."

He told the captain the entire story, including the particulars of the wager. "So, you see, I really do need to send her another letter. Or at least, make sure one gets delivered to her in the event the last one was intercepted by her mother or..." He let the comment trail off as he lifted a shoulder.

Crossing his arms over his chest, St. John began to chuckle. "You have left me wondering three things, young man," he said when his expression of amusement finally cleared. "First, are you prepared for how much this poor girl is going to..., nay, *already* despises you?"

Marcus furrowed his brows. "That bad, huh?"

"Second, have you a ring you can arrange to have delivered to her? And someone who can be trusted to make the delivery and see to it she is the recipient?"

About to answer in the negative, Marcus thought about the question some more. "I'd have to send them a letter, of course," he hedged, thinking he could prevail upon his younger sister, Beatrice, to do the honors. He could trust her. She'd have to make a special trip to London, but she would probably welcome the opportunity to visit the capital. She could even stay at Pendleton House.

"And third, this young lady sounds like the consummate gambler. However did you find someone who could so easily make a wager which only she could win?"

Rearing back at hearing the captain's assessment, Marcus scoffed. "What do you mean?"

The captain waved a bejeweled hand. "Don't you see what's happened here? She made the terms of the wager so she won no matter what happened in the gardens. She either walked away free and clear, but if she got caught, like she did—"

"We both did."

"—then she either gets a husband or she gets blunt. You, however, lose no matter what happened."

"I didn't lose, Captain," Marcus argued. "I *want* to marry her. And I may have..." He clamped his mouth shut, now wishing he had never mentioned anything to Viscountess Pettigrew.

"Go on," Captain St. John urged.

Marcus winced. "I made sure we were discovered."

Shaking his head back and forth, as if he was trying to understand the young man's claim, he said, "What? You waved your arms about? Made especially loud kissing noises? Announced it at the top of your lungs?"

"No, no, no, no," Marcus replied in frustration. "I arranged with Lady Pettigrew to discover us. So Miss Fitzsimmons would be..." He stopped speaking when he saw how the captain's eyes rounded in horror. "What?"

"You made arrangements for *ruination?*" St. John asked in disbelief. He dropped his head back on his shoulders and cursed softly.

"Something like that," Marcus admitted. "I wanted to ensure Miss Fitzsimmons would marry me."

"This... Lady Pettigrew. Is she a decent sort? Trustworthy?"

Marcus winced. "I've only just learned since coming on this trip that she is in fact one of London's premiere gossips and that she provides information to some news sheet called *The Tattler*."

A low whistle sounded from the captain. " Even *I've* heard of *The Tattler*. Might have even read an issue or two this past year." He shook his head. "Oh, you've gone and done it, young man."

"What? Done what?"

"Made a deal with the devil, you did. And now you'll be paying for it, probably for the rest of your life."

Marcus glanced overboard, halfway tempted to jump. No matter what happened to him, though, Lucy would still be left ruined. "How do I fix this?" he asked in dismay. "I don't want her to hate me—"

"Too late for that," St. John remarked.

"I did manage to get a letter off to her as we were leaving the docks, but I've no way of knowing if she ever received it. Apparently, even if it was delivered to her house, it's possible it was intercepted by her mother or..." He paused.

"Or?" St. John prompted.

"Her brother. Viscount Reardon."

St. John gave a start. "Reardon?" he repeated.

"Yes, Lord Reardon."

"Christopher Fitzsimmons, you mean? The army captain?"

Marcus gave a shrug. "I heard he fought the frogs on the Continent. I remember him from school, but he's older than us, so I was never friends with him."

The captain held up a staying hand. "But... you've met him? Recently?"

Nodding, Marcus said, "At the Weatherstone ball. A few nights ago. I asked him for permission to court Miss Fitzsimmons."

Swallowing, St. John's attention was captured by the sound of splashing water beyond the starboard railing. "So... he's alive?"

Momentarily confused, Marcus said, "Well, he was at the ball. Although he looked as if he might have eaten a bad lobster roll. He took his leave not ten minutes after I spoke with him."

"He gave you his permission?"

"He did," Marcus affirmed.

St. John chuckled softly. "Well then, this should work out after all," he murmured.

"What do you mean?"

"Reardon is an honorable gentleman," St. John commented. "If he's aware of what's happened, he'll set things right, and if he's not... you'll want to be sure to send him a letter. Apprise him of the situation, and tell him you'll be back in two years to collect his sister."

"Just like that?"

The captain scoffed. "Well, you might beg a bit."

Marcus hung his head. "I really wish Miss Fitzsimmons wouldn't hate me in the meantime, though."

Huffing softly, the captain patted him on the shoulder. "I plan to put into port at Valencia. I have some cargo to deliver, and our cook likes to take on some special ingredients he claims can only be found there." His expression suggested Doyle Watson might have had a different reason for wanting to stop at that particular port, but it wouldn't have mattered. One of the reasons he had such a loyal crew was due to the amount of space in the hold devoted to their food stores. Nothing would be gained by starving his men. They worked far better and longer on full stomachs.

"So I could send my letters from Valencia?" Marcus asked with some excitement.

"I'll do you one better. I know someone there who

could possibly act as a courier for you. See to it your letters to Reardon and Miss Fitzsimmons are delivered personally," St. John offered. "I might have a missive or two of my own I need delivered as well," he added, his voice sounding as if from far away.

"I would pay him, of course," Marcus replied. Although he didn't have a lot of extra money, he did have some gold his older brother had given him to use in an emergency. The small purse was sewn into the lining of one of his waistcoats.

St. John once again chuckled. "Write your letters tomorrow," he instructed. "Have them ready by tomorrow night, and I'll see to it they're given to a courier along with strict instructions."

"That soon?"

"It's only about twenty hours before we reach Valencia," St. John confirmed.

"Thank you, Captain," Marcus said, darting to the side when a cascade of water shot up from the starboard side of the ship.

"Seems we have a whale escorting us," St. John said with a grin. "A sign of good luck if I ever saw one. Now, off to bed, young man."

Marcus nodded and hurried to the companionway as another spout of water shot up, barely missing St. John as he made his way to his cabin.

If a whale was indeed a sign of good luck, then Marcus hoped they would see more of them. He needed all the luck he could get.

CHAPTER 13
A CAPTAIN'S RECOLLECTION

moment later

Once Captain John St. John had closed the door to his cabin, he leaned against the wooden slab and cursed softly.

Christopher Fitzsimmons was still alive!

Moving to his nightstand, St. John pulled out a bottle of brandy and poured a finger's worth into a small glass. About to put the bottle back in the cabinet, he instead reopened it and took a quick sip.

How could the viscount have survived his bullet wound to the belly?

St. John had been there at Waterloo when the young captain had been shot by a frog, the bullet penetrating his mid-section. He remembered watching in horror as Christopher Fitzsimmons doubled-over, fell off his horse, and landed with a *thud* on the wet battlefield.

He was sure the man was dead before he hit the ground.

The small regiment of soldiers, part of one of the two armies of the Seventh Coalition dispatched against French troops led by Napoleon himself, had gamely continued their fight, pulling their captain's body into the center of their circle and resuming their shooting among shouts and curses until the fire from the French had finally ceased.

St. John wasn't there because he was in the British Army, but rather because as a Foreign Office operative, he had been dispatched with a missive for the captain.

He had been a minute too late. Probably an entire day too late when he thought about the events of that battle. Had he been able to locate Captain Fitzsimmons when he was expected to rendezvous with him the day prior, the heir to the Reardon viscountcy wouldn't have taken a defensive position on the battlefield. He would have been on the outskirts, his band of soldiers kept at the ready but ordered not to engage unless absolutely necessary.

As the only son of Christopher Fitzsimmons, Viscount Reardon, the junior Christopher was meant to be spared. He had unknowingly inherited the viscountcy when the senior Christopher died unexpectedly a fortnight prior to the battle. St. John carried the updated orders as part of the tranche of documents he had been entrusted with as a spy.

Worse, St. John knew the younger Christopher had set his sights on a particular young lady to be his future viscountess. The second daughter of a Spanish nobleman, Lady Maria Paloma was beautiful, clever, and anxious to wed the English aristocrat.

Probably because she wanted to be free of her father.

José Antonio Arístegui de Benavides, seventh Conde of Albacete and a widower, had accepted an invitation to spend a few months at a country estate in Kent the year before. He had brought his daughter along in the hopes she might be betrothed before he returned to Spain, and, if he found a particularly well-off English widowed aristocrat in search of a husband, he was willing to remarry as a means to shore up his dwindling accounts.

St. John knew all this because he had been the one to transport them from Spain to England aboard *The Fairweather.*

Although St. John hadn't been present for their introduction at a house party in Kent, reports from those in attendance said Christopher and Maria's initial meeting was rocky at best, the young man showing more interest in her than she did in him.

A few weeks later, they met again during a *soirée* in London. Something had obviously changed, for it was rumored a betrothal had been arranged only a week before Christopher was dispatched to the Continent. A wedding occurred sometime before his departure.

The conde and his daughter returned to Spain, expecting to return to England when Christopher sent for her.

• • •

t. John sat on the edge of his bed and remembered how he had delayed his own return to British shores when that battle—the last of the Napoleonic Wars—ended. Knowing he had failed in his mission even as England succeeded in taking out the French forces, St. John made his way to where Lady Maria Paloma Silvestri y Arístegui de Benavides and her father were staying near Madrid to share what he had witnessed.

He would never forget the brave face Maria had displayed upon hearing the news of what had happened to Christopher. How her lower lip trembled as tears filled her eyes. How she had stood steady and tall until he had taken his leave of the count's apartments and, disguised as a Spanish sailor, made his way back to British shores and the life of a sea captain.

In the meantime, the count had taken his daughter to a villa in Valencia, a palatial house vacated by another aristocrat, to live out his days as a widower. Maria had promised to mourn the man she had been married to for less than a month.

When St. John paid a call during his last time in Valencia two months' prior, he soon learned she had kept her word. Dressed in a black bombazine gown and a black veil, she was still mourning a man who, according to Marcus Higgins, was miraculously alive.

So why hadn't Christopher Fitzsimmons sent word to her he still lived?

Perhaps he had, not knowing Maria and the conde were no longer in Madrid.

John St. John finished off his brandy and settled under the bed linens. The solution to Marcus Higgins' need for a courier seemed obvious as he dozed.

Who better than Lady Maria Paloma Silvestri y Arístegui de Benavides? She could deliver herself to the wounded viscount along with the letters.

Excitement growing at the realization he could reunite the two young aristocrats, St. John grinned as he fell asleep.

CHAPTER 14
A DREAM DISTURBS IN A MOST DELIGHTFUL WAY

eanwhile, in a certain young lady's bedchamber in Reardon Manor

Having read Marcus' letter for probably the tenth time since climbing into bed, Lucy Fitzsimmons finally turned down the candle lamp on the nightstand and fell asleep.

Although she rarely remembered her dreams upon waking the next morning—nightmares might leave her with a nasty memory—the one she experienced a few hours before dawn had her wishing she could remain sound asleep for the rest of her life.

For whenever had she experienced something so glorious as what Marcus Higgins did to her?

She wasn't sure when or how he had joined her in her bed, or even if it was her bed. The linens were soft, the mattress quite comfortable. He had settled his body next to hers while kissing her hair, her forehead, her eyelids, and finally her lips.

His fingers deftly undid the buttons on the front of her night rail, which she didn't mind in the least. She felt warm—too warm—and the cool night air felt good against her skin.

When the flat of his hand smoothed the cotton fabric off her shoulders to expose one breast, she inhaled softly, knowing the nipple had pebbled into a hard bud. The other, chafing beneath her night rail, wanted out as well. Apparently Marcus knew it, for he used his warm hand to free it, soon covering it with his mouth.

Her entire body seemed to come alive as his tongue flicked over her nipple. When he pulled away slightly, he blew cool air over it.

"Do you like honey?"

The question hadn't sounded the least bit odd at the time. "Of course," she had whispered, watching as he lifted a small pot of honey from the nightstand. He dipped a finger into the golden liquid and then swirled a dollop onto one breast.

She inhaled sharply and did so again as he coated the nipple of the other in the sticky sweet goo. He touched the tip of his finger to her lips, and she pulled it into her mouth. Using her tongue, she licked the remains of the honey from it, purring when he slowly pulled it out.

When his mouth descended once again on one of her breasts, she speared the fingers of one hand through his hair. She needed to hang on to something as he suckled the honey from her nipple. The sensations he created with his tongue and lips had her entire body ripening in a way she had never experienced before.

Every single nerve ending seemed to come alive all at once.

When he moved to the other breast, she cried out as his teeth took the hard bud and bit it slightly.

"Apologies, my lady," he murmured before she felt his mouth give up its hold on her. She was about to put voice to a sound of protest, but his lips were soon kissing her all the way down the front of her body, leaving a trail of cool moisture behind.

"Whatever are you doing?" she remembered asking, her voice breathy when she felt the cotton of her night rail slide up her thighs as his body moved farther down hers.

"I wish to taste your honey," he whispered.

Lucy couldn't remember having spread her legs for him. Couldn't remember having tilted her hips to expose her quim to his questing tongue. Perhaps he had been the one to do it, for she felt hot hands beneath the globes of her bottom, thumbs spearing the dark curls at the top of her thighs. Something there was throbbing with an ache she had never felt before, and she wished he would touch it. Rub it.

He did that and more, his tongue flicking and licking, his lips suckling it until she was on the verge of something monumental. When his tongue delved into her most private place, a spasm took hold of her entire abdomen, setting off a slow wave of pure pleasure unlike anything she had felt before.

She grasped both sides of his head with her hands as a means to hold on, sure she was drowning with each crashing wave. She wasn't even aware of how she sobbed, of how she begged for more and then begged for it to end because she simply didn't know any better.

And then all at once, Marcus was above her, his manhood replacing the space where his tongue had been.

His initial push into her was so slow, she lifted her hips of her own accord. Whatever he had been doing, she now wanted more. The sense of fullness when he was finally completely seated inside her helped somewhat, but she wanted the motion that had sent her insides into molten lava only the moment before.

He lowered his face, his forehead touching hers as his lips captured hers in a sweet kiss. Sweet, for she tasted honey as well as her own ambrosia.

"I love you. I have always loved you," he whispered. Then he began to move, pulling out of her and pressing into her, quickening his movements until he was thrusting and retreating so quickly, she could barely hang on.

She was hanging on, though, her hands gripping the sides of his chest, her thighs pressed into the sides of his, her feet hooked together at his back. The dusting of curls on his chest—she hadn't even noticed it before—tickled her nipples with each thrust until the sensation changed into something more intense. Something growing quite pleasurable. Something so wonderful she could only lie back and allow it to consume her.

When he suddenly ceased his movements, his face displayed a grimace of what looked like pain. She felt heat penetrate her insides. He collapsed atop her a second later, his head landing on the pillow next to hers.

Sliding her hands to his back to embrace him, Lucy held on until she felt his body slacken, and he rolled completely off of her.

She glanced over to see his eyes were closed. His chest, rising and falling as his breathing slowed, was damp with perspiration. The scent of musk and citrus tickled her nostrils, and she moved her head closer to his and inhaled.

"Is it always like this?" she asked in a whisper.

"Do you wish it to be?"

"I do."

"Then it shall be. Every night if you'd like." There was a long pause before he added, "Can you wait for me? Can you wait two years?"

She sighed in disappointment. "Oh, I will if I must."

"I can hardly wait to marry you, Lucy," he said before kissing her temple.

"I love you, Marcus Higgins," she whispered, feeling bereft at the loss of his heat and the weight of his body on hers.

She was soon tucked against his body, though, warmth at her back, a heavy arm draped over her waist, and a hot hand holding one of her breasts.

Sleep had barely descended on her when light disturbed her eyelids. Before she could put forth a word of protest—what was Marcus thinking to leave her bed so early?—her lady's maid's greeting of "Good morning" had her wide awake.

Sitting up with a start, she stared at Persimmon. Glancing about the bedchamber as if she expected to see Marcus in all his naked glory, Lucy scoffed and collapsed back onto her pillow.

She lifted the bed linens and stared down the front of her body, not at all surprised to see her night rail bunched around her middle.

Glancing over at the letter still on the nightstand, she decided she would have to read it before going to sleep every night.

Every night for two years.

CHAPTER 15
A COURIER ACCEPTS AN
ASSIGNMENT

*M*eanwhile, *at the Port of Valencia*

Although he hadn't planned to be part of an entourage when it came to paying a call at the palatial villa where the Conde of Albacete had set up residence the year prior, Captain St. John agreed to allow both Marcus Higgins and Frank Turnbridge to join him. Meanwhile, Sinclair and Hornsby set off with the cook, promising to help Watson haul his purchases back to the ship in exchange for a tour of the town.

Forgoing the uniform he usually wore at sea, St. John had opted to wear the clothes he did when he was acting as an operative for the Foreign Office. Dressed in leather breeches, a red waistcoat, and a navy wool top coat, he appeared as any European gentleman might. In place of a tricorn, he wore a short top hat. Tasseled black boots and black leather gloves completed his look.

The three made their way to the center of town,

easily negotiating the cobbled streets once they had regained their land legs.

Upon reaching the villa, Marcus gave a start. "From what you described yesterday, this is better than what I expected," he remarked, his gaze following the ornate plasterwork decorating the tops of the arches along the front of the building. St. John had told them during dinner that he thought the conde's residence was a perfect example of "elegant rot," a building that might have at one time been a masterpiece of architecture and decorative arts but was now barely livable.

"Looks can be deceiving," St. John warned. "If we're allowed in, you'll see what I mean."

Frank and Marcus exchanged curious glances at the same moment a liveried footman opened the tall front doors.

"Captain John St. John to see the Lady Maria Paloma Silvestri y Arístegui de Benavides," he said in perfect Spanish, handing a card to the servant.

The footman waved them into the large foyer. From the marble floors beneath their feet to the gilded ornamentation on the walls to the chandelier dripping with crystals above them, no expense had been spared in the original decoration. A wide marble staircase led to the first floor. However, a closer examination of the plastered walls showed cracks, and the drapes outlining the windows appeared faded, the velvet threads bare from sun rot.

"I think I see what you mean," Frank said in a hoarse whisper, his gaze taking in the painted ceiling. In this part of the villa, the high ceiling went all the way to the top, and from the water stains scattered about one corner, it was apparent the roof leaked.

As his gaze wandered down to one of the walls—the evidence of water damage was most apparent along an especially prominent crack—an argument in Spanish could be heard somewhere near the top of the stairs.

"The lady is in residence," St. John murmured. "And she is not happy."

Marcus dared a glance at the top of the stairs. "But she is a beautiful woman, if that is indeed her," he whispered. A young lady garbed in a black gown stood near the top step, waving her hands about in a frantic display of frustration. Her hair, wrapped in an elegant chignon and secured with a jeweled comb, was nearly as black as the bombazine gown she wore.

"That's her," St. John said, inhaling deeply. "Far thinner than when I last saw her, though," he added in worry. "She thinks we are someone else," he murmured, his brows furrowing as he tried to overhear whatever she was saying to the footman. At no point had she directed her attention on the three of them.

"Who?" Frank asked.

"Whoever owns this villa," the captain said, his gaze indicating he was still listening to the woman's angry tirade. "Apparently, she is no longer welcome to live here."

"What about her father?" Marcus asked in a whisper. "Doesn't she live here with him?"

"Good question," St. John murmured. He straightened when Maria finally halted her angry words and directed her attention on him.

"Hola, dama Maria," St. John said, bowing deeply.

Frank and Marcus exchanged quick glances before they, too, bowed.

"Captain St. John?" she said in English. She grabbed the bannister and quickly descended the majestic staircase, her slippered feet on display as she held up her slim gown with her free hand.

"I would be heartbroken if you hadn't recognized me," the captain said, moving to intercept her at the bottom of the stairs so he could take her hand to his lips. He pretended not to notice her chapped hands or how her collar bones showed in relief above the bodice of her gown.

"I am not blind, Captain St. John," she replied, her dark brows furrowing as she glanced first at Marcus and then at Frank. "If you have brought me potential husbands, you must know I am still in mourning for my Christopher."

St. John chuckled softly. "These gentlemen are two of my passengers. I am taking them to Roma for their Grand Tours," he replied. "Marcus Higgins..." he paused to wave in the young man's direction. "And Frank Turnbridge. They are both sons of earls," he explained.

Maria dipped a curtsy as Marcus rushed up to take her hand to his lips. "My lady," he murmured.

Frank followed suit, holding onto her hand far longer than necessary. "Lord Reardon is a very lucky man," he said.

Maria blinked, her dark brows furrowing as she turned her gaze on the captain. "What is he saying?"

"Christopher is alive, my lady," St. John stated, aiming a quelling glance in Frank's direction. He waved to Marcus. "This young man is betrothed to his sister, Lucy, which is how I learned of it."

Maria rushed to stand before Marcus, her eyes wide. "You have... you have *seen* him?" she asked in disbelief, gripping one of his hands. "Christopher Fitzsimmons? Captain Fitzsimmons?"

"*Sì*, my lady," he replied. "I spoke with him not even a week ago," Marcus assured her. "At a ball. When I asked his permission to court his sister," he explained.

"He was... well?"

Marcus furrowed a brow. "Well, he was... alive," he replied. "He looked a bit pale, but I think it was because he had eaten a bad lobster roll."

Maria appeared confused for a moment, her gaze going to St. John before she rushed to stand before him. Her subsequent words were said in Spanish in a combination of frustration, anger, relief, and happiness, many of them punctuated with punches to his arms and shoulders and finally a hard slap across his face.

Both Marcus and Frank recoiled in shock and then displayed matching expressions of confusion when she wrapped her arms around the captain's neck as tears erupted. A litany of what sounded like apologies soon followed.

"I must go to him," she said between gasps for breath. "You will take me?"

St. John aimed an arched brow in Marcus' direction. "I cannot, but there is a ship bound for London in port right now," he replied. "The captain plans to leave in the morning. If you'd like, I can see to it you have your own cabin."

She let go her hold on him. "I must be on that ship," she stated.

"I can arrange your passage," he assured her. "But… what about your father?" he asked, his voice lowered to almost a whisper. He had been expecting the aristocrat to make a grand entrance at any moment.

Maria dipped her head. "He has died," she replied. "Almost two months now. After you were last here."

St. John displayed a look of sorrow. "I'm so sorry," he whispered, even though he almost felt relief on her behalf. He was sure the conde had reached the point where he would have sold Maria into slavery as a means to make some blunt.

"I am not," she said on a huff, her tears quickly abating. "He spent all of my inheritance. I have no dowry," she added. "No money. No butler. No—"

"I can see to your passage to London," St. John interrupted. "Give you what you'll need to get to Lord Reardon's house. You can be there within the week."

She stared up at him. "*Gracias*," she whispered.

St. John nodded. "There is a favor you must do for this young man, though," he said as he waved to Marcus.

Maria directed her gaze on the young man. "*Favor?*" she repeated, suspicion evident in her voice.

"I need you to take letters for me to Lord Reardon's

sister, Miss Lucy Fitzsimmons, and to Lord Reardon," Marcus said. "And one needs to be posted to my sister."

"You'll act as a courier," St. John stated. "I have a missive for Lord Reardon, as well."

"Letters for Christopher's father?" she asked, her brows once again furrowing.

St. John inhaled sharply, immediately understanding her confusion. "Remember, Christopher's father died before he fought the French," he explained. "It was the reason I was dispatched to Waterloo. Christopher is Viscount Reardon now."

Her eyes rounded. "So... I am a viscountess?" she asked softly. Relief sounded in her voice.

"You will be," St. John confirmed. He dared a glance at the footman who was watching them from the top of the stairs. "You were angry with someone when we arrived," he said. "What has happened?"

Tears once again filled Maria's eyes. "A messenger arrived before you did. I have been told I must leave. This villa has been sold to become a... a hotel, I think it is called," she explained, obviously uncertain about the English word she used.

"Then you must be on the ship to London in the morning. If you would like..." He glanced up again, noting the servant was no longer watching them. "I can help you with your trunks. See to it you are safely on board," he offered.

"I will pack my trousseau right now," she replied, turning to climb the stairs. "The rest is already packed."

"Pray tell, how many trunks will you take, my lady?" Marcus asked.

Three sets of eyes turned to regard him in surprise. He shrugged. "She's a woman. I have two sisters, so I know there will be more than one trunk," he said in his own defense. "There are only the three of us," he added sheepishly.

"Four. I have four trunks," she replied, already racing up the stairs. "Two valises. Mayhap three. And a wooden crate."

The men all seemed to roll their eyes in unison.

"A wooden crate?" Frank repeated under his breath.

"We'll need a cart," Marcus remarked.

"We shall return for you soon, my lady," St. John called up to Maria.

"I will be ready," she replied, before disappearing from view.

St. John lifted his hands to his hips and sighed. "Well, it seems we have a cart to locate."

"But at least we have a courier," Marcus said.

The three took their leave of the villa to search for a means to transport the lady's luggage to the port. It seemed they had some work ahead of them that afternoon.

CHAPTER 16
A GRUMPY EARL READS HIS CORRESPONDENCE

Meanwhile, in the southernmost tip of Staffordshire

The newly minted Earl of Greenley, Max Higgins, stared out his study window and contemplated what the next year held in store for him. Besides taking on the mountain of debt his father had built with his incessant gambling, Max would be taking a wife.

Not the one he had planned to wed. Patience Seward, daughter of the Earl of Eversham, had thrown him over in favor of a marquess, it seemed.

Not that he could blame her exactly. She had to know the dire straits he was in. Had to know she wouldn't be able to live the life she had grown accustomed to as the oldest daughter of an earl.

If he had secured her hand in marriage, her dowry would have effectively wiped out most of the Greenley earldom's debt. The income from the farms would be enough for them to live comfortably. Not extravagantly, though. Not enough so she could have her own modiste and pin money to spend on anything she liked. Not so she could travel to Bath or Brighton or Paris or wherever it was aristocratic ladies liked to spend their holidays.

Just thinking about Patience with another man had him feeling grouchy. Grumpy. Short of, well, *patience*.

"The post has arrived, my lord," Bertram announced from the study's doorway. The butler held a silver salver in one hand, its surface littered with envelopes. In the other, he carried a cup of tea on a saucer, two biscuits perched on the edge.

"You are my least favorite person in the whole world," Max said dryly, mostly to see if he could disarm the unflappable servant.

"Of course, sir," Bertram replied calmly. He had learned the year before not to take anything his master said to heart. "However, today I bring you only correspondence."

Max straightened so fast in his worn leather chair, he nearly hurt his neck. "No invoices? No bills? No—?"

"None, sir. Only letters."

The butler set the salver and saucer before Max, who had to clear away some space on his messy desk.

"You might be my favorite person in the whole world," Max murmured as he lifted one of the envelopes from the salver.

"Very good, sir. If there is nothing more?"

Max waved a dismissive hand before undoing the folded corners of one envelope. His last comment hadn't even coaxed a small grin from the butler, and it bothered him that he was bothered by it.

He quickly opened the letter, his gaze going to the bottom.

Marcus? Whatever was his younger brother up to now?

> *Dear Max,*
>
> *I am writing to inform you of my arrival in London. Frank Turnbridge and I have completed our arrangements for our Grand Tour and leave for Rome on The Fairweather on the morrow.*

Max scoffed lightly, a stab of jealousy bringing a curse to his lips. Even if there hadn't been a war with France when he was of an age to go on a Grand Tour, there wouldn't have been funds for it. At least Marcus had the wherewithal to secure his inheritance from the earldom's solicitor the year prior and make arrangements for investments that might see him live in comfort for the rest of his life.

> *I accepted an invitation to the Weatherstone ball. Should the opportunity arise, I intend to secure a promise of marriage from someone for whom I have felt affection since, well, as long as I can remember.*
>
> *I shall spare you her name as I suspect it will only make you grouchier than usual. I should not want you firing Bertram since I rather doubt there are any other servants in Staffordshire looking to be your butler.*

Screwing up his face in a grimace, Max barked out a curse. "Damnation," he added in a quieter voice. His brother knew him too well. As for the identity of the young lady, Max didn't have any idea to whom Marcus referred. The only reason he would be grouchier is if he learned Marcus was intending to propose to Madeline Thistlewaite.

> *I do hope Lady Madeline agrees to be your wife. If anyone can tame the beast, it is her. Please be nice to her. She will be an excellent mother and a welcome addition to Higgins House.*
>
> *I will write when I can and hope the post works from Rome and Athens.*
>
> *Sincerely yours,*
> *Marcus*

Settling back into his chair, Max glanced up at the ceiling and considered his brother's words. *I'm always nice to Madeline*, he thought.

He opened the top drawer of his desk and dared a quick peek inside to ensure his mother's sapphire ring was still there. He planned to give it to Lady Madeline later that night. Her parents, the Earl and Countess of Bravershead, had invited him for dinner. Even though it would require a trip of over three miles to reach the earldom's summer estate, he had decided it best he accept the invitation and secure Madeline's hand in marriage.

His gaze darted back to the salver. The red wax seal

on the back of it wasn't familiar to him, and he examined it closely before he popped it off and unfolded the letter.

> *Dear Lord Greenley,*
> *You are no doubt surprised to hear from me. My memories of you are from our time spent in Hyde Park as children, vexing our nurses with our raucous play and language unbecoming of the titles we have since inherited.*
> *I will spare you condolences as I have reason to suspect they would not be welcome.*

"The man has that right," Max muttered under his breath.

> *A letter from your brother Marcus arrived today for my sister, Lucy.*

Max blinked, his gaze going to the letter Marcus had sent him. Then it dropped to the bottom of the letter he was reading.

> *Rt. Hon Viscount Reardon*

Chuckling, Max suddenly realized what his brother meant. Even though their late father might have hated Matthew Fitzsimmons, Viscount Chamberlain, and everyone with whom he was related, Max knew better than to hold the viscount completely responsible for the sins of his father. Besides, Christopher Fitzsimmons was merely the nephew of Chamberlain and had nothing whatsoever to do with the Foreign Office. At least, he didn't think he did. He was fairly sure the viscount had been a captain in the British Army.

During last night's ball at Lord Weatherstone's mansion, my sister made a wager with your brother, the repercussions of which are either a payment of ten thousand pounds to my sister or marriage to her.

I am aware the funds may not be readily available and that a marriage cannot occur until Marcus is back on British shores, which given his itinerary, will apparently not be for another two years.

Although Lucy is of the opinion she is owed the amount of ten thousand pounds, I reviewed the terms of the wager with her to discover this is an "either or" situation.

For purposes of the immediate future and given the dire straights in which she has been cast—her reputation is irrevocably stained due to their discovery together in the Weatherstone gardens—I told her to consider herself betrothed.

In the event your brother Marcus does not intend to wed her, might you know if he is in possession of the ten thousand pounds?

I ask only out of concern for my sister, Lucy, as she is now betrothed to him.

I look forward to your earliest reply.

Sincerely yours,

Christopher Fitzsimmons

> *Rt. Hon Viscount Reardon*
>
> *Post scriptum: Please understand I hold no ill will toward you or your brother. Except for their discovery by Lady Pettigrew, this situation is almost entirely my sister's fault since she set the terms of the wager.*

Max stared at the last few lines of the letter for several seconds before shaking his head. Obviously Lucy Fitzsimmons had set the terms of the wager before his brother had had a chance to ask her for her hand in marriage. Otherwise, there would not have been a mention of ten thousand pounds.

On the one hand, he could understand how Reardon thought his sister at fault, but on the other, his brother had been with her in the gardens—kissing, no doubt—and they had been discovered. He winced at seeing the name of the viscountess who had caught them. Lady Pettigrew's ability to spread gossip was legendary.

Not about to wait to reply, Max immediately pulled out a sheet of stationery, sharpened his best quill, and dipped it into the ink pot.

> *Dear Lord Reardon,*
>
> *Your letter is both welcome and a surprise. I do recall our times in Hyde Park with fondness, especially since I was probably the loudest of all of us. I believe your use of the word "vex" is understated. My late mother saw to the hiring of no fewer than four nurses for the six years before I was turned over to the tutors.*
>
> *I cannot say at this time if my brother Marcus is in*

possession of ten thousand pounds (I rather doubt it), but I can assure you he has seen to investing what he has not taken with him on his Grand Tour with one Gregory Grandby, a financier with some reputation for earning large sums on behalf of his clients. His investment opportunities range from canals and structures to something which is eventually supposed to replace our coaches. I have not the imagination to think what that might be.

As to the betrothal, please allow me to assure you that he does indeed wish to marry your sister, Lucy. I have in hand a letter from him sent the day of his departure from London apprising me of his intent to secure a promise of marriage from her, although he would not share her name directly because he thought it would make me grouchy. It does not. I do not share my father's hatred for Lord Chamberlain.

Should the two be wed upon his return to England, I will welcome your sister into our family. I hope to do so with my wife, as I intend to propose marriage to Lady Madeline Thistlewaite later this evening. (You may have come upon her brother in London as he is on the hunt for a bride there. Your sister was on the list.)

I shall now consider my brother betrothed to your sister.

Sincerely yours,
Maxwell Higgins
Earl of Greenley
Post Scriptum: You might consider taking your

sister with you when you next expect to place a wager. It sounds as if she's crack at them!

Scattering sand over the letter, he swished it about until the ink was dry. He dumped it back into the container, folded the letter, applied his wax seal on the corners.

"Bertram!" he called out.

A moment later, the butler appeared.

"See to it this is posted. I'm going to change for dinner, and I'll need the coach ready to leave in an hour."

"Very good, my lord," the butler said, taking the missive.

"With any luck, I'll be sharing my brother's status as a betrothed man when I return."

"Very good, sir. And if you are not lucky?"

Max aimed a glare at the servant. "Then I'll not return."

He had a difficult time suppressing a grin at seeing Bertram's attempt to hide his reaction of surprise.

CHAPTER 17
A SURPRISE PASSENGER IS LOADED WITH THE LUGGAGE

*L*ater that day

Leasing a donkey, a cart, and a driver turned out to be far easier than Marcus Higgins expected. John St. John's ability to speak Spanish had the hired cart pulling up to the villa only an hour later, the men sitting on the back with their legs dangling over the edge.

Two other locals walked behind, a promise of pay once the crate and trunks were loaded onto the ship enough of an incentive for them to leave behind a game of dice.

"What do you suppose she's taking to London?" Frank asked when the footman opened the front doors to the villa as the cart stuttered to a halt.

"Probably everything she owns. Everything her father owned, or what's left of it," Marcus replied. He felt sorry for the young woman. Before his older brother had taken over the running of the Greenley earldom, there were times Marcus imagined what might become of him and his sisters when his father died and left them all penniless.

The only two entailed properties of the Greenley earldom were Pendleton House in Mayfair and Higgins House and its farms and a village in Staffordshire. There was little left in the way of unentailed properties that could be sold to shore up the earldom's accounts.

Marcus had thought he might one day have to work as a clerk in London to earn his living. He could stay in the capital. Or, if he couldn't find employment there, he could join his brother in the southernmost tip of Staffordshire and live in Higgins House. Work in a nearby village. Even if he packed up everything he owned, it would barely fill a trunk.

Lady Maria was still rushing about somewhere upstairs when they entered the foyer. As promised, four trunks were stacked up and ready to be loaded. The wooden crate, not as large as Marcus feared, was missing its lid, but a quick peek inside had him giving a start.

"What is it?" Frank asked, joining Marcus.

"Looks like a bed," he replied before his eyes rounded. "For a very small person."

"A bassinet," Frank said in a whisper. "Could be for a dog."

"Looks old," Marcus remarked. "It was probably hers."

"Why take it to London, though? They have bassinets there."

"Sentimental reasons, I suppose," Marcus said with a

shrug. "Probably wants to use it for her and the viscount's children when she has them." He dipped his head. "This isn't right," he murmured.

"What do you mean?"

"Putting a woman on a ship. By herself? No protection? She doesn't even have a lady's maid," he said in a whisper.

Frank dared a glance up the stairs, his brows furrowing as he watched the woman in question open a valise and reach in. A moment later, she briefly held a bundle before returning it to the valise. She seemed to say something to it before rising and hurrying away.

He turned and regarded the crate once more before he sighed. "You want to go back to London, don't you?" he asked.

Marcus screwed up his face in a grimace. "Would you hate me if I left you to travel with Sinclair and Hornsby?" he countered.

Shrugging, Frank said, "I suppose not. They have the same itinerary as we do," he replied. "If you go back, I'll have the cabin to myself. I won't have to listen to you snore. And you can provide protection for..." His eyes widened before he chuckled. "She's eventually going to be your sister by marriage."

Marcus punched his friend's arm. "She is," he agreed. "I need to speak with the captain of *The Pembroke Prize*. Find out if he has room for me aboard ship."

"And if he doesn't?"

Marcus allowed a shrug as he glanced down into the wooden crate. "I can try being a stowaway."

The laborers saw to loading the trunks as Maria descended the stairs with the last two valises. She had changed into a dark red gown, and a black mantle hung from her shoulders.

When St. John rushed up to take the valises from her, she held onto one of them. "I will see to this one," she said.

"As you wish," he replied. "Are you sure you have everything?"

She nodded, although her eyes were bright with unshed tears. "I do not know what I would have done if you had not come today," she whispered.

St. John furrowed his brows. "Surely someone would have taken you in," he replied.

"Me, perhaps," she said. "But not him, too." She indicated the valise she held.

"Him?" St. John repeated. "What? Have you a puppy in there?" he asked, thinking she might have an ankle biter like so many aristocratic women in England did.

She shook her head and reached down to open the bag. He peered down, his eyes rounding at seeing a baby wrapped in a blanket. "Who...?"

"Christopher José Antonio Arístegui de Benevides Fitzsimmons," she said proudly.

St. John blinked. "When...?"

"A few days after you were last here," she replied.

He scoffed, remembering how she had seemed rather plump the last time he had paid a call at the villa. "And here I thought you were eating too many cakes at tea time," he remarked.

"I wish I could eat cake," she replied on a sad sigh. "No money, though."

"I'll see to it you have enough food for the trip to London," he assured her.

"I do wonder what Christopher will think of him?" she said as they made their way to the cart. "He is his heir."

St. John winced. "I rather doubt he'll be allowed to inherit," he said in a quiet voice. "Our laws of inheritance require—"

"Marriage, yes," she said, holding up a rolled parchment. "We wed before he had to leave for war."

Staring at her in disbelief, St. John shook his head. "I'll be damned," he muttered. When he noted how her expression changed to one of worry, he held out a staying hand. "He'll be thrilled," he assured her. "I almost wish I could be at Reardon Manor to see for myself when you introduce this one to his father," he added with a chuckle.

He helped her up to the bench seat so she was next to the driver, the valise on her lap. After the wooden crate was loaded, the laborers helped to push the cart until it was moving and then walked behind it as it rumbled over the cobbles and down to the dock.

An hour later, Lady Maria and her luggage were loaded onto *The Pembroke Prize*. The captain had accepted a reasonable bribe to see to it she always had a seat at his table for meals and arrangements once they reached London for transportation to Reardon Manor. A number of letters were stuffed into her reticule, their recipients and addresses clearly written on them.

"I'll have her there in three days," Captain Macintosh promised.

"She carries the future Viscount Reardon in that valise," St. John said in a low voice, not sure he wanted the rest of the crew to know there would be a baby on board.

"I'll have him there in three days as well," the captain said, chuckling even as he shook his head. "I don't know how you get yourself into these situations, St. John, but you are a better man than me."

Captain St. John merely shrugged. "I would normally expect a reward from this one, but considering I was the cause of the unfortunate situation, I feel it's only necessary I make it right," he explained.

The two shook hands and St. John made his way back to *The Fairweather*. A few minutes later, and he was in the wheelhouse, steering his ship out of port.

He had no idea he was short a passenger.

CHAPTER 18
A BROTHER'S PLAN IS PUT INTO PLAY

The following morning, Reardon Manor breakfast parlor

"Really, darling, if you keep frowning like that, you'll have permanent lines across your forehead," Jane Fitzsimmons said as she waved for the footman to refill her teacup.

Lucy looked up from her breakfast plate, expecting the comment had been said to her. Instead, her mother's attention was on her brother.

"I'm not frowning, Mother. I'm reading," Christopher countered, his gaze on that morning's *The Times*. He suddenly inhaled as he leaned forward. "Ah, here it is," he said with some excitement. "On page six."

"What's that, darling?"

"A betrothal announcement."

In the middle of chewing on a slice of toast, Lucy stopped moving her mouth and stared at her brother. She couldn't even repeat what he'd said with her mouth full, so she was glad when her mother did it for her.

"Betrothal announcement? Whose?"

"Lucy's, of course," Christopher remarked. "And Mr. Marcus Higgins, current heir to the Greenley earldom. These are so rarely done, it's quite good of the young man to have seen to its publication before he departed on his Grand Tour."

Lucy swallowed. Hard.

"What's this?" Jane asked, halfway out of her chair.

"Sit down, Mother," Christopher stated. "This is welcome news. Best wishes, Sister," he added, directing his gaze on Lucy.

"Thank you," she replied, although she wasn't sure an expression of gratitude was called for at the moment. They had discussed the situation, though. At length. Her brother's immediate solution seemed well-advised and well-timed, given there was another ball scheduled for that evening. Even if only half the aristocracy read the newspaper, word would spread quickly, perhaps even as soon as this afternoon's calls, and she would be spared further censure from the likes of Lady Pettigrew.

From where Christopher had found the ring he had given her the night before, she had no idea, but the single sapphire on a gold band was already on her finger. Although it wasn't unheard of to be gifted a betrothal ring, she knew it was uncommon. However, after telling Christopher of the ring Frank Turnbridge had given Marianne to secure their betrothal, he had apparently decided she needed one, too.

Despite several attempts to make her mother notice the bauble—she had waved it about as she reached for the cream-pot, tapped her fingers on the table as the footman refilled her tea, and even splayed her fingers on her chest when she leaned back—Lady Reardon's attention had been on other matters. Apparently, the cold eggs, the amount of fat in the ham, and the length of her day gown's sleeves had all of her attention that morning.

"Well, what does it say?" Jane asked. "You must read it aloud. All of it," she insisted.

Christopher leaned back and lifted the paper before him. He cleared his throat and recited, "Mr. Marcus Higgins, brother of Maxwell, Earl of Greenley, secured a promise of marriage from Miss Lucy Fitzsimmons prior to his departure to Rome to begin a Grand Tour. He will marry the only daughter of the late Christopher Fitzsimmons, Viscount Reardon, and sister of the current Viscount Reardon, upon his return to England. A gold ring, decorated with a sapphire of some value, has already been given to Miss Fitzsimmons as a parting gift. A wedding date has not yet been set."

Grinning broadly, he lowered the paper to discover Jane staring at Lucy in disbelief. When her gaze finally fell on the ring, she gasped and appeared as if she was about to faint.

"Why didn't you tell me?" she asked in dismay. She grabbed Lucy's hand in both of hers to examine the ring.

"I thought Christopher was going to tell you," she replied. "Since Mr. Higgins spoke with him at the ball. To gain his permission to ask for my hand."

Her mother sighed as she shook her head. "Well, this is certainly going to be the subject of interest in all the parlors in Mayfair today, I should think," she said with some excitement.

Despite being the subject of an article in *The Times*, and the probable subject of that day's gossip over teas up and down Park Lane, Lucy found she didn't care. Even if it meant she could attend that night's ball without fear of reprisals—without fear of having to stand with the wallflowers all night—she decided she didn't even care if her dance card was full.

She was officially betrothed to Marcus Higgins.

Even if *he* didn't know it.

After all, how likely was it he would see a copy of *The Times* where he was going?

None of his relatives would either, given the earl was in Staffordshire and his sisters didn't live in London.

Her brother's plan was brilliant. And brilliantly executed.

She could always beg off once Marcus returned to British shores. Publicly claim her affections for the young man had dimmed with his lengthly absence from London. She would no doubt have to forgo the ten thousand pounds he had promised in the wager, which had her feeling a bit used, but then she would be rid of the business.

It would serve Marcus right. A revenge of sorts for what he had put her through these past few days. Not that it was really his fault they were discovered. But he had accepted the terms of the wager.

Glancing over at her brother, Lucy noticed how he regarded his breakfast plate as if the food on it was poisoned. "What's wrong?" she asked in a quiet voice, fearing his heartburn had returned.

He gave a start. "I am merely reminded of my own marital status," he replied.

"We shall find you a wife this year," Jane said happily. "There are a number of fine young ladies who would be perfect—"

"I already have one, Mother," he stated, perhaps a bit too forcefully.

Jane sobered, her brows furrowing to make her appear far older than she was. "Are you referring to Lady Maria? That Spanish—?"

"Mother," he interrupted, the tone of his voice severe. "You will not speak ill of my *wife*," he stated.

Rearing back in her chair so hard she nearly sent it tilting backward, Jane stared at her son in shock. Her breath caught, and she seemed to struggle for air. When she glanced over at Lucy, her face screwed into a grimace.

"Did *you* know he married her?"

Lucy nodded. "They married right before he left for the Continent. About a year ago," she said nonchalantly.

"Then... then why isn't she *here?*" Jane asked, her manner indignant.

"Christopher wanted to completely recover from his wound before he sent for her," she replied, hoping she sounded reasonable. "And to make sure she would be welcomed here at Reardon Manor when she arrived."

She exchanged a quick glance with her brother, hoping she was doing him a favor with her words. After what he had done for her, it was the least she could do. "You will welcome her, won't you, Mother? Because if you don't, you might wish to have Christopher arrange for the dowager house in Somerset to be aired and staffed for you."

"Lucy," Christopher said in a whisper of warning.

"You wouldn't," Jane said, her eyes wide with fear.

Christopher arched his brows. "If you don't believe you could live under the same roof with Maria, then I will do what I must."

"You'd be close to Bath," Lucy said with some enthusiasm. "Why, you could take the waters every day and enjoy the... how did you put it? 'The elegant stupidity of private parties'?"

"That's enough, Lucy," Christopher said, noting how their mother's eyes had filled with tears.

"Please, don't send me to Somerset," Jane murmured.

"You will welcome Maria into this household? Allow her to be the lady of the house?" Christopher asked in a quiet voice.

Jane seemed to consider the query for a long time before she said, "She'll need help," she reasoned. "With doing menus and ordering the staff about," she added before she took a steadying breath. Her eyes suddenly rounded. "Her father won't be with her, will he?"

Christopher shook his head. "Given his age, I expect he'll remain in Spain," he replied. He wished he knew exactly *where* in Spain the two had settled. If he did, he would depart on the next ship to Asturias, Santander, or Cantabria, or if necessary, Valencia or Barcelona.

"With any luck, she'll be here in time for your anniversary," Lucy said hopefully.

"Thank you, Sister," Christopher replied. He pushed away from the table. "On that note, I shall go to my study. I have some correspondence to write."

Jane and Lucy watched him go before Lucy turned her attention back to her plate. "So, what gown will you wear to the ball tonight?" she asked brightly.

Her mother stared at her for a moment before a sob robbed her of breath. "I think the coquelicot would do nicely. I believe it will help put some color in my cheeks," she said. "As for you, perhaps we should pay a call on the modiste? See if we can't get you fitted for a gown with some color, now that you're a betrothed young lady."

Liking the sound of her new situation, Lucy dared a grin. "Pale blue, do you suppose? Or pink perhaps?"

"Both," Jane replied, arching a brow.

Smiling in delight, Lucy ate her breakfast, not the least bit bothered by the cold eggs or the fatty ham.

CHAPTER 19
THE FUTURE IN-LAWS MAKE
PLANS

The evening prior, on The Pembroke Prize

"I appreciate this, Captain Macintosh," Marcus said, bent from the weight of the trunk on his shoulder. He gripped the handle of his valise in his other hand.

"It seems I'm being taught lessons in chivalry on this day," the captain replied dryly. "Your cabin is rather small, but it's the only one left."

"I only need it for a few nights," Marcus replied.

"It's next door to her ladyship's," the captain added. "I'll show you." He led Marcus to the companionway.

"She doesn't yet know I'm doing this," Marcus said, allowing the captain to take the trunk once he was at the bottom of the steep stairs. "But she's going to be my sister by marriage, and I would feel terrible if anything happened to her."

"Understood," the captain replied. "Join me at my table for dinner," he said, opening the door to a cabin that was barely long enough to accommodate a bunk and the single table and chair. "Cook usually has it ready at seven o'clock."

"I look forward to it, Captain. Thank you." He paused, remembering what he had overheard at the villa. Maria apparently had no money, which meant she probably hadn't had much to eat. "Might your cook have something available in the meantime? Should the lady wish for tea or biscuits?" he hedged.

Captain Macintosh eyed him with suspicion. "I rather doubt there are biscuits, but I'm sure he has something to satisfy your hunger," he replied. "Galley's that way," he said, pointing down the corridor. "My dining room is up top."

"Thank you, Captain."

Marcus took a moment to move his trunk into place and pull a few items from his valise. He chuckled softly at remembering how he had struggled to pack for what he had thought would be a two-year trip. Instead, his entire time away from England would be no more than ten days.

He hoped he wouldn't regret the change in itinerary.

Moving to Maria's door, he knocked softly.

The lady opened it only a few inches, but when she realized who stood on the other side, she opened it wider. "Mr. Higgins? Has something happened?"

"My lady," he said, bowing before he reached for her hand to brush his lips over the back of it. "I wish to offer my protection. I will see to it you are safely delivered to Lord Reardon when we arrive in London."

Maria's eyes rounded. "But... Captain St. John will not wait for you. You will miss your—"

"I know. It's all right," he assured her. "I think I shall prefer to go to Rome with Miss Fitzsimmons rather than with Mr. Turnbridge."

"You are married?" she asked in confusion.

He shook his head. "Not yet, but that is part of the reason I must return to London," he said. "One of those letters I gave you—the one for Miss Fitzsimmons—was meant to reassure her that I would return to marry her. I think it best I do so now rather than later," he explained.

"Have you proposed marriage to her?" she asked, waving him into the cabin. The unmistakeable sounds of a baby's cooing came from the bassinet, and a tiny fist could occasionally be seen waving about above the edge.

"Not exactly, but given what happened before I left London, I certainly think we are betrothed."

Maria arched a dark brow. "Have you ruined her?"

His face darkened with his embarrassment. "In a manner of speaking," he replied. "I was caught kissing her in the gardens during a ball," he blurted. He waited until she was seated next to the bassinet before he took the other chair.

"Then you are as honorable as my Christopher," she said, lifting the babe into her arms. She settled it on her shoulder. "We were married before I left England."

"You're *married*?" he asked in surprise. From the moment they had discovered she had a baby, Marcus and Frank had assumed the child was born on the wrong side of the blanket. Given its age, there was no way to tell if it bore any resemblance to Lord Reardon.

She nodded. "Yes, of course. He insisted we do so before he joined his regiment," she explained. "I could have remained in England, I suppose, but my father was not welcome to stay, and I did not wish to be left with Christopher's mother, Lady Reardon." She screwed up her face in a grimace. "She does not like me. Because I am Spanish." She paused a moment. "She thinks I am bad *ton*," she added with a shrug.

Marcus winced, knowing there were many in the aristocracy who thought the same about his family given his father's gambling habit. "Well, she won't be the lady of the house once you get there," he remarked.

"She won't?" The woman's eyes rounded in confusion.

Realizing she wasn't familiar with the matter of how aristocratic households were run in England, Marcus considered how to respond. "As the lord's wife, *you* will be the lady of the house," he explained. "And since you have given Lord Reardon his heir, his mother is now the Dowager Viscountess Reardon."

Maria winced. "The English ladies do not like that title," she said. "Or living in dowager cottages, at least, I do not think they do from what I learned when I was in Kent last year."

Marcus chuckled softly. "Some don't, it's true. But others don't mind because they like having grandchildren." His attention went to the baby. Wide awake, the babe was attempting to look about the cabin, his head bobbing as he struggled to keep it up. "Do you call him Christopher?"

"*Sì*," she replied. "Would you like to hold him?"

His eyes widening, Marcus stammered for a moment before he said, "Yes, actually. It's been a long time." He leaned over to take the bundle from her.

"You have held a babe before?"

"Um, not really. I have a younger sister, but she's only a year behind me in age," he explained, his gaze locked with that of the baby. "I don't remember when Beatrice was this small. How old is he?" He settled the bundle into the crook of his arm, thinking the boy couldn't weigh more than half a stone.

"Almost... eight weeks now," she said, her attention on her mind's eye. "Fifty-four days."

"Does he have a nurse?" he asked suddenly, fearing they may have left a servant behind in the mad rush to load Maria's trunks onto the ship.

"There is no need. I see to him," she said proudly.

Marcus held the boy's gaze for several seconds, feeling almost jealous. He couldn't remember ever being held by his own mother, nor could he remember her holding Beatrice. They were only in her company a few minutes every day after they had eaten their dinners. "It must be difficult for you, though," he murmured, grinning when the babe gripped his forefinger with a tiny fist.

Maria angled her head to one side. "If you and Captain St. John had not come along when you did, I do not know what I would have done," she whispered, her brows furrowing as tears collected in the corners of her eyes.

He glanced up at hearing the catch in her voice. "But we did, and that's all that matters," he replied, chuckling softly when he realized the baby had fallen asleep in his arms.

"He likes you," she said with a watery grin.

"I'm going to be his uncle," he replied, a huge grin the evidence of his joy.

Maria's smile widened, and she tittered. "Then we must see to it Miss Fitzsimmons marries you," she said.

Sobering, Marcus nodded. "Yes, indeed," he agreed. Sudden hunger had his stomach growling. "In the meantime, let's see if I can't find us some food. You must be starving."

The slight shake of her head didn't deter him. He stood and placed the baby in the bassinet. "I'll return shortly," he promised. Giving her a quick bow, he hurried off to find the galley.

CHAPTER 20
A MISSIVE AMIDST THE BILLS

*T*he following day, Reardon Manor

Christopher had barely made it into the study when Peters appeared with that morning's post.

"Anything look important?" he asked as the butler set the salver onto the edge of his desk.

"There is one from Staffordshire," Peters replied. "I fear the rest are invoices, including this one from her ladyship's modiste." He arched a graying brow.

Rolling his eyes, Christopher took it and set it aside. "Mother and Lucy were there yesterday," he said on a sigh. "But I must say Lucy looked resplendent in her new gown. Blue becomes her."

"Ah, the belle of the ball?" Peters guessed.

Christopher chuckled. "In a manner of speaking. She is betrothed now."

Peters didn't display a hint of surprise, but then he rarely showed any emotion. "Lady Reardon must be very glad."

"Oh, she is," the viscount remarked, remembering how his mother behaved at the ball the night before. Despite a few old biddies remarking on the poor financial status of the Greenley earldom, Jane was quick with reminders that a new earl was in charge now. Surely the ledgers would show a profit before Lucy and Marcus exchanged their vows.

The butler took his leave of the study while Christopher opened the missive from Staffordshire. He gave a start upon seeing it was from Max Higgins. "Already?" he whispered, quickly popping off the wax seal with a thumbnail. The earl had obviously written as soon as he had received Christopher's letter.

He glanced over the words a moment in an attempt to decipher the masculine scrawl. Nearly as bad as his brother's penmanship, Max's writing was bolder, the letters larger.

When he reached the second paragraph, he sat up straighter.

I cannot say at this time if my brother Marcus is in possession of ten thousand pounds (I rather doubt it), but I can assure you he has seen to investing what he has not taken with him on his Grand Tour with one Gregory Grandby, a financier with some reputation for earning large sums on behalf of his clients. His investment opportunities range from canals and structures to something which is eventually supposed to replace our coaches. I have not the imagination to think what that might be.

"Clever young man," Christopher murmured, growing excited at the thought that by the time Marcus returned from his Grand Tour, he might have earned a reasonable sum of money. Gregory Grandby was a cousin of his godfather, Milton Grandby, Earl of Torrington, and had an excellent reputation among the *ton*.

As to the betrothal, please allow me to assure you that he does indeed wish to marry your sister, Lucy. I have in hand a letter from him sent the day before his departure from London apprising me of his intent to secure a promise of marriage from her, although he would not share her name directly because he thought it would make me grouchy. It does not. I do not share my father's hatred for Lord Chamberlain.

Feeling a good deal of relief, Christopher settled back in his chair and sighed as he continued to read.

Should the two be wed upon his return to England, I will welcome your sister into our family. I hope to do so with my wife, as I intend to propose marriage to Miss Madeline Thistlewaite later this evening. (You may have come upon her brother in London as he is on the hunt for a bride there. Your sister was on the list.)

I shall now consider my brother betrothed to your sister.

Sincerely yours,
Maxwell Higgins
Earl of Greenley

*Post Scriptum: You might consider taking your
sister with you when you next expect to place a wager. It
sounds as if she's crack at them!*

Christopher chuckled and tossed the letter to his desk. He had never met the woman mentioned in the letter, but he knew Lucy had danced with her zany brother, Viscount Thistlewaite, at a recent ball. Christopher could only hope her father, an earl, would see the potential in the Greenley earldom and not hold the sins of Max's father against him.

"Good news?" Lucy asked from where she stood in the doorway. "I heard you laughing."

He nodded. "Greenley writes that he considers you and his brother betrothed to one another," he announced. "And apparently you have dodged a bullet."

Lucy's eyes rounded. "What do you mean?"

"Greenley has proposed to Viscount Thistlewaite's sister, Madeline. Says he's here in London in search of a wife, and he thought of you."

Gasping, Lucy glanced to the floor. "No wonder he seemed so distant last evening. He didn't even ask me to dance," she said.

"This is exactly why Marcus saw fit to securing permission to marry you before he departed," Christopher said.

"Thank you for what you did," she said in a quiet voice. When she noted his look of confusion, she added, "The article in the paper? The ring?" she clarified. "Where did you get the ring, by the way?"

Christopher nodded to the door, and Lucy understood she needed to close it. "It's paste," he replied. "Good paste, but..." He shrugged. "Don't allow anyone to look too closely at it," he warned.

Tittering, Lucy moved to the chair in front of his desk. "So Marcus told his brother he intended to marry me?"

"He did," Christopher affirmed. "Which means... he's obviously been thinking of proposing marriage for some time," he said. "I know you're not happy with what's happened, but perhaps you could give him a chance upon his return. Don't just break off the betrothal before you spend some time with him."

"I won't," she replied. "I must admit, it's rather flattering to have a young man hold me in such regard."

Christopher grinned. "His execution could have been better planned, but it worked in the end," he remarked.

"I came to warn you about my gown," Lucy said, changing the subject. "Mother got a bit carried away yesterday..." She stopped when Christopher held up the invoice from the modiste. "Oh, dear," she whispered.

Chuckling softly, Christopher said, "It's all right. Two for the price of..." He glanced at the total and winced. "Three," he finished, his brows furrowing. "But you're set for the rest of the Season, are you not?"

"I am," she replied. "Have you heard any news from Spain?" she asked, her manner timid.

He shook his head. "I spoke with our uncle. He'll inform me if any word should come from Madrid. I spoke with the shipping company that employs Captain St.

John. He's the one who transported Maria and her father to England," he explained. "Turns out, Marcus Higgins is on his ship, but St. John isn't due back here in London for almost a month," he complained. "I've left word I need to speak with him when he does."

Lucy listened intently, remembering the letter Marcus had sent the day of his departure. "Do passengers ever speak with the captains of the ships they're on?" she asked. "Conversationally, I mean."

Christopher shrugged. "I did, but then I was an officer in the army. I ate dinner at the captain's table." His eyes suddenly widened.

"Would Marcus be eating at the captain's table?" she asked.

"He would indeed," her brother said in a whisper. "Probably all his passengers do. St. John... he's a..." He clamped his mouth shut, realizing he shouldn't be sharing information about the captain's other job with his sister. "A gossip," he quickly amended. "Apparently loves news of the goings-on in London."

"Well, if Marcus mentions having spoken to you, then St. John would know you're not dead. He might be reminded of Lady Maria. Perhaps he'll send word of her."

Christopher nodded. "From your lips to his ears," he murmured. "Marcus didn't know I was looking for her, though," he added, his momentary excitement abating.

Lucy angled her head to one side. "Chin up, Brother. It might be another month before you can speak with him, but you will eventually."

"In a month, I will have been married a year," he

responded. "If I don't learn her whereabouts by then, I will go mad."

Rising from her chair, Lucy leaned over the desk. "Don't be making arrangements for a bed in Bedlam just yet," she said. "A month is a long time."

Not about to argue, Christopher watched her depart the study. A moment later, he began writing cheques to cover the bills on the salver.

The modiste was the first one to be paid.

CHAPTER 21
THE FUTURE IN-LAWS
ARRIVE

he following day, Wapping

The sounds of distant shouts had Marcus giving a start, his head jerking up from the bunk in his cabin. The heavy weight resting on his chest squirmed, and he glanced down to discover he had fallen asleep with the future Viscount Reardon atop him.

A moment of panic passed before he remembered he had offered to take the babe for the afternoon to give Maria time to bathe and dress.

They were due to arrive in London at any moment.

Struggling to sit up in an attempt to not wake the baby, Marcus realized it was too late. The boy's eyes were already open.

"Hello," he said in a whisper.

From the uncertain look on the baby's face, he feared the boy was about to let out a wail. For the three days they had been on the water, the babe rarely cried, only doing so when he was hungry.

Although Maria would have been fine remaining in her cabin for the entire trip, Marcus had encouraged her to go topside a couple of times for fresh air and for a walk about the deck. He held the babe whilst she climbed the companionway, and then she took little Christopher from him once he was a few steps from the top.

They had eaten their meals with Captain Macintosh, enjoying tales of his adventures on the seas during the wars. At no point during their time in his dining room had the babe required undue attention, for he was usually sound asleep.

At the moment, his barely-there eyebrows seemed to scrunch together, and Marcus realized he was going to make a sound of complaint at any moment. He quickly rose from his bunk and hurried out of his cabin, relieved to discover Maria's cabin door was open and she was in it, calmly combing her long, black hair.

Already dressed in a sprigged day gown, one that wrapped in the front, she could have been any young lady. Although her skin was more olive-toned than that of an English miss, Marcus understood how Christopher Fitzsimmons could be attracted to the young lady.

"Did he give you any trouble?" she asked, holding out her arms to take him. At the sound of his mother's voice, the babe cooed softly and squirmed inside the blanket.

"Not at all. We fell asleep, actually," he admitted. "I can hold onto him until you finish your toilette," he offered.

"I will have my hair pinned up in a moment," she said, turning to regard her reflection in a hand mirror she had propped up against the wall of cabin. "I cannot tell you how nervous and excited I am to return to my Christopher," she said, twisting her long hair into a bun atop her head.

Marcus watched in fascination. Although he had two sisters, one older and one younger than him, they had both had a lady's maid to see to their hair. "I may be more nervous than you," he remarked. "I have no idea how Miss Fitzsimmons will greet me."

Maria tittered. "She might slap you across the face, but I expect she will follow it up with a kiss to your lips," she said. Marcus had told her all about the wager, the kiss in the gardens, and how the Ladies Pettigrew and Reardon had discovered them. He might have also let it slip that he had arranged for Lady Pettigrew to come upon them as a means of securing a promise of marriage from Lucy.

Wincing, Marcus took the other chair and settled the babe on his lap so he could see his mother.

"Do you still have the letters I gave you?" he asked.

"I do."

"I just realized my letter mentions I won't be returning to London for two years, so..."

"When you deliver me to Reardon Manor, you will come in with me and ask to see her. If she is not there, or if she refuses, then I will give her the letter," Maria explained. "If she cannot or will not afford you an audience, you will return on the morrow and kiss her."

Marcus furrowed his brows. "How am I going to kiss her if she won't see me?" he asked.

"I will see to it," she said, a prim grin appearing to lighten her face.

Grinning, Marcus watched her push the last of her pins into place. In the few days since they had left Valencia, the woman looked far healthier than she had when they had first found her, the color in her face due to the anger and frustration she felt at the situation in which she found herself. Although she had looked beautiful in the black widow weeds she had worn in Valencia, she looked far more stunning in the brighter day gowns she had worn on the trip.

"I appreciate your help," Marcus said.

At the sounds of shouts, they both turned to the porthole window. "Is this London?" Maria asked, rising to see for herself.

"The docks, actually. London is still a few miles off," he replied. Although the ship was still moving, it had slowed considerably.

"I will feed the baby now," she said. "So we are ready to go when the ship stops."

Marcus knew he would have to line up a porter and see to a hackney and a dray cart to handle all the trunks. "I'm going to speak with the captain," he said.

An hour later, the three departed *The Pembroke Prize*, joining the throngs of passengers and crew that rushed about on the docks.

· · ·

*I*t was nearly two more hours before they reached Mayfair, the sun about to set beyond Hyde Park. The sense of excitement Maria had felt when they were finally ensconced in a fairly clean hackney—Marcus had rejected the first one for its horrid odor—had settled into anticipation. Next to her, Marcus nervously fisted and spread his gloved hands. Behind them, a dray cart of dubious repair was stacked with her trunks and trundled along, its wheels noisy on the cobbles.

Marcus had paid a street urchin to deliver a message and his luggage to Pendleton House with word that he would be moving in for the foreseeable future. With any luck, Lucy would be moving in once they were wed. Until then, the housekeeper would have to continue seeing to the menus and to running the household.

When they finally stopped in front of Reardon Manor, Maria inhaled softly. "It looks the same," she whispered nervously.

"You've been here before?"

She nodded. "Only the one time. Christopher wished to show me his house."

He helped her down from the hackney, taking the babe from her. When he didn't immediately give him back once she was on the pavement, he said, "I have a feeling you're going to have your arms full in a few minutes."

Grinning in delight, she hooked her hand into his

elbow as they approached the front door. The butler opened it before they had a chance to use the boar's head knocker.

"Might Lord Reardon be in residence?" Marcus asked. "Also, we'll need some footmen to unload some trunks from the dray cart out front."

The servant stepped aside, his brows furrowing upon seeing Maria. "Might I tell him who is calling?"

About to search for a calling card, Marcus said, "Marcus Higgins. Tell him I have a surprise for him." He absently bounced the babe in one arm.

His brows rising, the butler nodded and disappeared into one of the rooms off the main hall.

"I think I'm more nervous than you are," Marcus claimed, stepping aside to allow a pair of footmen to pass.

"I am not nervous," Maria countered. "I am happy, though. My Christopher is alive."

The subject of her words emerged from his study as if shot from a canon. "Higgins?" he called out. He slowed his steps, his attention going from Marcus to Maria. "Maria," he whispered, making his way to her as if in slow motion.

"Christopher. You are *alive*," she said, rushing to him.

The two collided several feet in front of Marcus, and he watched in wonder as the viscount wrapped his arms around his wife and held her close, his murmurs too quiet to hear. Tears collected in the corners of his eyes when the two finally parted enough to stare at one another.

"I've been so worried. When you didn't answer my letters."

"I never received any letters, but Father moved us when we were no longer welcome in Madrid. I thought you were dead because—"

"Captain St. John told you," Christopher guessed, his forehead pressed to hers.

"Yes. When Mr. Higgins told him he was to marry your sister and that he had asked your permission, then Captain St. John knew you were not dead and came for me." She waved to Marcus. "He was kind enough to offer protection. To escort me to you, even though it meant giving up on his Grand Tour," she explained.

Christopher directed his gaze on Marcus, his expression of confusion changing to one of humor. "You, sir, might have been a source of consternation for this household for the past... nine or ten days, but I find I am in your debt," he said as he approached, his hand held out.

Marcus shook it. "Apologies for the mess I caused. I only wished to ensure Lucy would marry me," he said.

His attention going to the bundle Marcus held at his shoulder, Christopher asked, "What have you there?"

"Oh!" Marcus said, repositioning the babe so he faced the viscount. "Lord Reardon, allow me the honor of introducing you to Christopher José Antonio... something de Benvides Fitzsimmons," he stammered. "Your son and heir, my lord."

Blinking, Christopher stared at the babe and then at Marcus. He turned to discover Maria at his elbow. She reached for the baby, taking it before turning to place it into Christopher's arms. "Christopher José Antonio *Arístegui* de Benevides Fitzsimmons," she stated.

"My son?" he asked in a whisper. He swallowed as he stared down at the babe. "How...?"

Marcus was quick to say, "He is fifty-nine—"

"Sixty days old today," Maria said proudly. "Father met him before he died."

For a moment, a cloud seemed to pass before Christopher's face. "I am sorry for your loss."

She shrugged. "We were no longer welcome at the villa in Valencia, and so it was best," she said in a quiet voice.

Christopher used his free arm to wrap it around her shoulders and pull her close. "I cannot tell you how relieved I am you are all right," he murmured. "You are well?"

"I am," she said, "Thanks to Mr. Higgins and to the cook on *The Pembroke Prize*. He fed us well," she said with a grin.

The two footmen entered with a trunk held between them.

"The mistress suite," Christopher stated, realizing they were waiting for orders. He turned to Marcus. "I would have Peters send for Lucy, but she and our mother are attending a card party this afternoon. I don't expect them back for some time."

Disappointed but not surprised, Marcus nodded. "Would it be all right if I paid a call on the morrow?"

"Of course. She should be home most of the day,"

Christopher said. "If you'd like, I can put in some more good words for you," he said. "It's the least I can do given what you've done for me."

Marcus considered his offer. "Lady Reardon carries a letter I wrote to Lucy. She knows what to do with it." He turned to her. "There's no need to post the one to Beatrice. The ring I mention in that letter is here in London," he said.

"What of the letter you gave me for my husband?" she asked.

His brows furrowing, Marcus considered what he had written and decided it was still valid. "Give it to him," he said. "It was easier to write it than it would be to say it aloud," he added.

"Where will you go?" the viscount asked, worry crossing his face.

Marcus straightened. "Pendleton House. I've sent my trunk ahead with word that I'll be staying there for the immediate future. The few days I was there before departing for Rome has me thinking I shall be the only one left of the family living there."

"Is it staffed with servants?"

He nodded. "A few. More than enough for me," Marcus said with a shrug.

"And beyond that?"

He took in a deep breath. "Well, that all depends on Miss Fitzsimmons," he said. "If she agrees to marry me within the month, I have funds and arrangements for a tour of the Kingdom of the Two Sicilies. I think it would make for a good wedding trip, don't you?."

Christopher chuckled. "She'd be a fool not to agree to your terms," he said. "We can draw up the contract once you have her convinced," he added.

"Then I shall call again on the morrow," Marcus said, bowing. "My lady," he said, reaching to take her hand to his lips. "It has been an honor."

Maria placed her hands on either side of his head and drew it down until she could kiss his forehead. "I am glad to finally have a brother," she said happily.

"A third sister is the charm," he replied.

Christopher watched as Marcus took his leave, stepping aside to allow the footmen to carry in another trunk. "Come, my sweet. Let's get you two settled," he said with a watery grin. He dipped his head until his nose was nestled in the babe's tuft of dark hair. "Do they always smell this good?"

Maria wrinkled her nose. "Not always," she replied. "He probably needs his nappy changed."

Christopher hefted his son onto his shoulder before offering her his arm. Despite the tears that streamed down his face, he happily said, "I'm a father."

Maria giggled in delight.

CHAPTER 22
EVIDENCE OF AN ARRIVAL IS NOTED

*L*ater that night

"I do hope your brother didn't wait for us for dinner," Jane remarked when she and Lucy approached Reardon Manor, the pavement from the coach illuminated by a gas lamp Peters had lit on their behalf. "I didn't realize Lady Norwick was going to include a supper this evening."

When Lucy didn't immediately respond, Jane paused before lifting the knocker and noticed the girl's attention was on the bit of lawn that fronted the terrace. "What is it?"

Lucy furrowed a brow. "The grass is all trampled," she murmured. "And it looks as if something heavy was sitting on it for a time."

"I'm sure Peters will have an explanation," her mother said at the same moment the door opened to reveal the man in question.

"Good evening, my lady," the butler said, stepping aside to open the door wider.

"Well, do you have an explanation for why the lawn is trampled?"

Peters furrowed a brow before he directed his gaze out front. "Oh, uh, a delivery was made for Lord Reardon earlier this evening," he stammered. "It took the footmen some time to... to move it."

Jane and Lucy exchanged quick glances. "A delivery?" Jane repeated.

"Something in a trunk," Peters said, helping them with their mantles. "He had it taken straight up to his bedchamber." Before they could ask after the viscount, Peters added, "His lordship has had his dinner and has retired for the night. He asked that he not be disturbed."

"Is he all right?" Lucy asked, worry in her voice.

"Oh, he is right as rain, my lady. He said he will see you at breakfast."

Jane and Lucy both reacted with curious glances but made their way through the hall and to the stairs. "We're off to bed as well, Peters."

"I'll see to locking up the house. Good-night, my lady." Peters stood watching from the vestibule, his lips quirked in a grin of self-satisfaction.

Starting tomorrow morning, things would be very different at Reardon Manor.

CHAPTER 23
A REUNION IS SWEET

eanwhile, in the mistress suite

When Christopher made his way through the connecting dressing room to her bedchamber, Maria glanced up and gave him a brilliant grin. He wore a long dressing robe, and from what she could see under the hem, she surmised he was naked beneath the navy velvet.

"He's nearly full," she whispered, the babe noisily suckling at her breast. One of his fists, now pressed against her breastbone, occasionally pounded on her as she gently rocked the chair in which she sat near the fireplace.

Christopher knelt next to the chair and kissed her cheek. "Does he always make this much noise when he eats?" he asked in a whisper, his amusement apparent.

"Only when he's very hungry."

"Is the chair comfortable enough for you? If not, I can have—"

"It's fine, darling," she whispered, cupping her free hand against his jaw. From how smooth his face felt, she knew he had shaved only moments ago. The scents of citrus and musk surrounded him. "I like it, and I think he does, too. In fact, I think I shall like sitting in it even if I'm not holding Christopher."

The father nodded. He'd had a footman bring the rocking chair down from the nursery during dinner. Despite it having been nearly two decades since it was last used by her nurse to rock Lucy, the chair seemed in good shape.

"He did so well on the ship. He hardly cried," she murmured. "I think he liked the motion of it."

"What shall we call him?"

Maria gave a start. "Do you object to his name? I thought—"

"Oh, Christopher is fine. It's perfect," he assured her. "But to alleviate confusion here in the household, I wondered if we should call him... Antonio, perhaps?"

"Shouldn't I be calling you Reardon?"

He screwed his face into a grimace. "I like how you say my name," he claimed.

She turned her attention back to the babe. "Antonio it is," she whispered.

Placing a hand on the top of his son's head, Christopher rubbed the boy's forehead with his thumb. The move didn't seem to bother the babe, for he continued to nurse for another minute before his lips slowed their sucking and he fell asleep.

"Finally," Maria said. She was about to rise from the

chair, but Christopher held a hand to her shoulder. "Let me do it," he whispered.

Maria watched as he stood and lifted the babe to his shoulder. She had thought he was going to place the boy in his bassinet, but he patted the babe's back for a moment until a burp came forth.

"Careful, he might—"

"It's fine," he assured her. He kissed the top of the baby's head before leaning over to place him in the bassinet. When he had him covered with a blanket, he turned to discover Maria standing next to him. Her dressing gown, still untied from when she had been nursing, was open wide enough reveal one breast and most of another.

"I have missed you so much," he whispered, pulling her until she was pressed against the front of his body. "I have been worried sick—literally—every day since..." He couldn't continue when she speared her fingers through his hair and pulled his head down. Her lips captured his in the first kiss they had shared since her departure from England nearly a year ago.

Christopher returned the kiss. Returned it and set about starting another and yet another as he walked them to the edge of the bed. When he ended one of them, he asked, "Are you able...? I mean, can we...?"

Maria stared up at him. "Make love, do you mean?"

He nodded.

"Of course. If we do not, I shall be very..."

She nearly let out a yelp of surprise when she was

suddenly off of her feet and sitting in the middle the bed, the robe only covering her arms and back.

"Disappointed," she finished as she stared up at her husband.

"Then I shan't disappoint," he said. He kissed her once more, pushing her down with a warm hand on her shoulder. When she was on her back, Christopher covered her body with his own, trailing kisses along her collarbones and the tops of her breasts, over her belly down to the apex of her thighs.

"I almost took you at the dinner table," he whispered hoarsely.

Maria spread her legs apart, apparently well aware of what he intended to do. "I thought you were going to when you said you were ready for dessert. I have been ready for you since then."

"I was thinking it when the first course was delivered," he countered in between kisses to the tops of her thighs.

Even before his tongue made contact with the soft folds of her quim, already glistening with her anticipation, he heard her pleas and slid his hands along the inside of her thighs. When her torso rose from the bed, he lowered his head and flicked his tongue across her engorged womanhood. Her body trembled in response.

Another flick had her begging him to impale her, and the last had her saying his name in a sigh so soft, he nearly obliged her. But he waited until he heard her sob before capturing the bud with his lips and suckling it.

When he felt her body shiver and shake beneath him, he pulled his own body up and over hers.

Thrusting his manhood into her welcoming cocoon, he nearly lost control in the process. He forced himself to hold on, to deny himself the release his body had demanded since the moment he had placed the babe in the bassinet and took her in his arms.

She lifted her thighs and gripped his, her calves wrapping around his buttocks to trap him. Feeling the undulating waves and then the sudden clench on his manhood was his undoing, and he stiffened as the intense pleasure took him under.

When he collapsed atop her, allowing a long groan of satisfaction, Christopher barely understood her litany of Spanish, the words strung together in one continuous murmur. When her fingernails speared his hair and scraped his scalp, they sent skitters of delight beneath his skin. He couldn't help the curse that followed, couldn't help but say, "I love you," even as he begged her to stop.

Finally succumbing to sleep, his body went limp.

*M*aria stared at the canopy above as she struggled to catch her breath. This had been nothing like their first night together in a bed. Nothing like that awkward coupling that had been as clumsy as it was uncomfortable.

Having barely given him permission to join her in her bed, Christopher had simply claimed her on that warm spring night nearly a year ago. His body had been so heated, she felt as if he had branded her as his own at the same moment he took her virtue.

Although they had spent a few hours in bed together, she had awakened the following morning to discover him gone.

Their reunion over breakfast had been cordial. Confusing. It was only when they were in private when the newly commissioned captain showed any interest in her during the house party in Kent.

That is, until he had proposed marriage, given her a ring, and announced their betrothal to all in attendance at a farewell dinner given in the conde's honor in London at Mivart's Hotel.

That had been their last night together.

Learning her father had given his permission for the marriage more than a week before Christopher had asked for her hand had Maria wondering why the captain had waited so long to propose.

Had he doubted her commitment to him? Had he thought her fast because she hadn't turned him away when he had come to her room that warm spring night? Had he doubted his own desire for her? Had he learned her father couldn't offer much if anything in the way of a dowry?

When she finally confronted him after their last dinner together, after the port had been drunk in the dining room and the ladies had departed the parlor, he had admitted, "I wanted to ask you when I first met you, but I knew you would deny me. I wanted to ask the night

I took your virtue, but I did not think it appropriate. I wanted to ask you the moment I saw you again here in London, but I thought it best to give you time to feel affection for me. For you to realize I would make you a happy wife."

His words had been true. He had given her the time she needed for her affection to grow. For her regard for him to make itself apparent to them both.

Then he pulled a paper from his waistcoat. "I saw to a special license so we can be wed before I leave for the Continent. If you'd like, we'll marry in the morning."

They made love later that night, a coupling far different from their first night together. Even now, her body seemed to remember how he had pleasured her. How the quiet, intimate act had left them both feeling satiated and replete.

They had married the following morning. By that afternoon, they were both on board ships bound for the Continent.

Although Christopher would have preferred she remain in London and live at Reardon Manor, she reminded him she was not liked by his mother. She hadn't even met his sister. Besides, she wished to return to her childhood home to pack her things. She would await for word from him regarding arrangements for her travel when the war was over.

A fortnight later—only a week after Napoleon's forces had been defeated by the coalition armies—John St. John had arrived in Madrid, bringing news of Christopher's apparent death on the battlefield.

Despite how easy it would have been to take a lover in Spain, Maria had turned away those who showed an interest in her, proudly displaying the bauble and marriage certificate she had been given as proof of her marriage to an English viscount. Besides, she felt duty-bound to mourn him. She was his wife.

Ever since Captain St. John's most recent visit five days ago, she had felt a combination of anger and dismay at learning the young viscount was still alive. Why hadn't he sent for her? Why hadn't he come to Spain to collect her?

Reminded she and her father weren't where they were supposed to be helped settle her somewhat, but surely news of his recovery could have been forwarded to Valencia by someone.

For the entire trip from Spain, she had wondered how Christopher would behave when they were reunited. How she would react upon seeing him again.

Well, I certainly have my answer now, she thought as she held Christopher's head between her hands. The side of his face rested between her breasts, and she could feel his steady heartbeat against her belly.

If she hadn't been nursing his heir, his seed might have taken root, and she could bless him with a spare heir in the new year.

Her thoughts once again strayed to Captain St. John. If he hadn't taken on a passenger who happened to mention Viscount Reardon's name in passing, he wouldn't have known Christopher was alive.

Poor Marcus, who had only thought the best of

Viscount Reardon—probably because he had given his permission to court his sister—had been so attentive and so honorable in seeing her delivered to her husband.

Reminded of the letters she carried on his behalf, she was about to extricate herself from Christopher's hold when she felt his arm tighten around her.

"Please, don't go," he whispered. "Ever."

She tittered softly. "All right," she replied in English. "But I have Mr. Higgins' letters for both you and your sister, so I must make her acquaintance on the morrow."

Christopher mumbled something incoherent before adding, "Breakfast. I'll introduce you at breakfast," he whispered.

Suddenly weary from her travels and from what he had done to her only moments ago, Maria pulled the bed linens over them as best she could and nodded off to sleep.

CHAPTER 24
AN AWKWARD INTRODUCTION

he following morning, ground floor, Reardon Manor

Ensconced in the front salon, Lucy regarded the bright white sheet of stationery she had pulled from the drawer of her escritoire and considered whose letter she was going to reply to first.

There was one from a cousin, a recollection of her trip through the Lake District the month prior as part of her wedding trip. Another was from her aunt Christine, an older lady who was spending her Season in Bath so she might enjoy the waters.

The last was the missive from Marcus Higgins. Every morning for almost a week, she had reread the letter in an attempt to discover if her reaction to his words had changed. Every morning, she had decided she was still just as annoyed as the moment she had read it the first time.

At least it no longer incited anger or the desire to behead one of the marble busts in the hall.

About to take a quill in one hand, she paused when she realized she was no longer alone.

She quickly stood. "How do?" she said, staring at the gorgeous young woman who stood on the threshold, her hands clasped together at her waist. Her black hair was caught up in a bun atop her head, and her olive skin seemed to glow from within. Her gown, a style similar to those currently in fashion in England, was of a fabric and pattern Lucy didn't recognize.

The woman dipped a curtsy. "It's very good to meet you." The words were said in accented English but were easy to understand.

"And you," Lucy replied. Realizing there was no one to do an introduction, she added, "I am Lucy Fitzsimmons."

Stepping forward, the young woman held out a hand. "I am Maria Paloma Silvestri y Arístegui de Benavides Fitzsimmons, second daughter of the late José Antonio Arístegui de Benavides, seventh Conde of Albacete." She paused a moment. "But you may call me Maria."

Lucy suppressed the urge to giggle at hearing the litany of names even as her eyes rounded. "Maria," she whispered. "Christopher's Maria, are you not?" she asked, her excitement growing. She belatedly curtsied.

The woman nodded.

"However did you get here?" Lucy asked, noticing the woman held an envelope in one elegant hand.

Maria displayed a momentary look of confusion. "A hackney, I believe is the name of the equipage?"

Lucy glanced out the window, half expecting to see a hackney parked in front of the terrace. "This morning?" she said in confusion. About to ask if she had come all the way from Spain in a hackney, Lucy realized that would have been impossible.

"No. Yesterday. On *The Pembroke Prize* and then in a hackney," Maria clarified.

Remembering Christopher's absence when they had returned home the night before, Lucy realized Maria must have arrived whilst she and her mother had been at the card party. The trunk Peters had mentioned had no doubt belonged to her.

A delivery for Christopher, indeed!

"Have you seen him, then? My brother, I mean?"

"Oh, yes. I have seen him," Maria replied with a wave of her free hand. "All of him," she added, a brow arching in delight.

Thinking at first she misunderstood the young woman, Lucy felt heat color her face. She waved to one of the upholstered chairs. "Would you like to take a seat?"

Maria nodded and made her way to the chair Lucy indicated. Meanwhile, Lucy stuck her head out of the salon in search of Peters. When she saw only a footman, she called out to have tea delivered.

Moving to join Maria in another chair, Lucy took a seat and regarded her with a pleasant expression. "So... my brother told me only a few days ago that you and he had married," she said. "Last year?"

"We did," Maria confirmed. "And then I thought him dead because Captain St. John told me he was, and then a few days ago, the captain found me and told me he wasn't dead."

Lucy's eyes widened. "How awful." No wonder Christopher hadn't heard from her.

Maria's brows furrowed. "It was not to discover he wasn't dead," she countered.

Lucy realized her comment had been misconstrued. "I meant, how awful that you were ever told he was dead at all," she amended. "Although there were times we feared he might die. His wound—"

"Oh, I have seen it," Maria said, her body shivering in disgust. "He is all better now, though."

Lucy felt the heat return to her face. "Since you're married to my brother, that means you're my sister," she said. "I've always wanted a sister."

Maria grinned. "I have always wanted a brother, which is why I've come to you before seeing anyone else this morning."

Confused, Lucy said, "Me?"

Maria held out the envelope. "I am to deliver this to you and to offer further explanation should it be required."

Taking the missive as if it might explode in her fingers, Lucy immediately recognized the masculine scrawl on the front.

The Hon Miss Lucy Fitzsimmons
Reardon Manor

Mayfair

She stared at Maria. "Are you... are you acting as a courier for someone?" she asked.

The young woman nodded. "For this letter, yes. I was happy to deliver it on his behalf."

Lucy unfolded the letter, her attention immediately going to the signature at the end.

Marcus Higgins

She glanced up. "Did he give this to you? Personally?"

"He did. Four... five days ago. In Valencia," Maria replied, grinning as if she found the situation amusing. "When you have finished reading it, I will tell you more."

Lucy was about to read when Peters appeared with the tea tray. "I will see to serving," Maria stated. "So you can read." The grin she aimed in Peters' direction suggested she was already acquainted with the butler.

"Good morning, Lady Reardon," Peters said. "Breakfast will be served at half-past the hour. Would you like chocolate?"

"Sì, gracias."

Peters nodded and took his leave while Lucy was torn between reading the letter and staring at Maria. "Lady Reardon," she murmured. "I'm so sorry I didn't realize it sooner."

Maria shrugged. "I have been for nearly a year, and yet Peters is only the second person to call me that."

"Who was the first?"

Dipping her head as she poured the tea, Maria said, "I will tell you after you read the letter."

Lucy scoffed, but did as she was told. Nearly everything Marcus wrote matched what he had already written in the missive that was opened on her escritoire. It was almost as if he hadn't thought the original was delivered.

"So... you have met Mr. Higgins?" Lucy asked as she accepted a cup of tea.

"Indeed. He is a fine young man. Very generous and very kind," Maria said before she took a sip of tea. "He loves you very much."

Lucy stared at the woman who had been her sister-in-law for almost a year now. "You make it sound as if you have spent a good deal of time in his company."

"That's because I have."

A stab of jealousy had Lucy giving a start. "Oh?"

"His letter was written before he changed his itinerary, you see," Maria explained.

Lucy glanced down at the letter to reread the line about how he would return in two years to marry her. "Is he coming back to England earlier than planned?"

"Oh, he already has. He provided protection for me when we departed Valencia a few days ago. He did not want me traveling alone, you see, especially given little Christopher." She paused a moment. "Antonio, rather."

Her eyes widening at these two bits of news, Lucy stared at Maria. "Marcus Higgins is back in London?"

"He is. He lives at Pendleton House. Where you will be the lady of the house should you agree to marry him."

Lucy blinked several times. "Little Christopher... is he your baby? I'm an aunt?" she asked in disbelief.

"For sixty-one days," Maria replied, tittering. "Reardon is over the moon, of course. And so good with him. He already knows how to hold him. How to burp him," she added.

"That might be because he used to do that with me, when I was still in the nursery," Lucy replied. "He's five years older than me, you see. Where is...?"

"Oh, to alleviate confusion, we're to call the babe Antonio," Maria explained, using the same words she remembered Christopher saying. "He's upstairs in the mistress suite. I fed him awhile ago, so he's sound asleep now, much like your poor brother," she said, her face blooming with color.

Lucy grinned. She might have raced up the stairs to meet her nephew, but the thought that Christopher was in the mistress suite had her remaining where she was.

"Mr. Higgins will pay a call on you today," Maria stated. "Sometime this afternoon."

Sighing, Lucy said, "Thank you for telling me."

Maria nodded and said, "If I might make a suggestion?"

"Please do," Lucy encouraged.

"When he arrives... after he has kissed your hand and you have curtsied—performed all the pleasantries—you must slap him across the face and then kiss him."

Lucy blinked. "I may have already decided to do that. How ever did you know?"

Maria tittered. "It is what *I* would do." She sobered.

"I almost did it to your brother yesterday, but he could not help what happened."

Sipping her tea, Lucy had a thought. "So... Captain St. John found you... to tell you my brother was still alive, but... how did *he* learn of it?"

"Because Mr. Higgins told him. If he hadn't been aboard *The Fairweather,* St. John wouldn't have learned the truth. He wouldn't have come for me and arranged my passage to London." Her face paled. "In another few days, I would not have been at that villa. My father and I were not welcomed at my sister's castle near Madrid, and so we had moved into a villa in Valencia. The owner had been a friend of the family for many years, you see, but it was sold shortly after father's death, and I was told I had to leave. If Captain St. John had not found me when he did, I don't know where I would have gone. A widow with a baby?" She shrugged.

"How awful for you," Lucy whispered. She stared at Maria for several seconds, the realization of her words slowly sinking in. "Christopher has been... *ill* with worry for you. It was only this week he thought Captain St. John might have spoken with you. Might have told you he was dead."

"He did," Maria replied. "He did not do so out of malice, of course, but rather because he did not wish me to discover it from someone else, or from reading it in a news sheet."

"There you are," Christopher said, beaming as he entered the salon. He proudly carried his son on his shoulder. He hurried over and dropped a kiss on Maria's cheek as Lucy came to her feet.

"Good-morning, sleepy head," Maria whispered.

"Me or him? Because he's still sound asleep."

Maria aimed a grin in Lucy's direction. "He wasn't at six o'clock this morning," she murmured.

"May I hold him?" Lucy begged.

"He's heavy," Christopher warned.

"Mr. Higgins said he's half a stone, whatever that means," Maria whispered.

Lucy inhaled softly when the babe was placed into her arms. "Oh, I want one," she said on a sigh.

Maria and Christopher exchanged quick glances.

"That can easily be arranged," her brother remarked. "Today, in fact. Marcus Higgins is going to pay a call this afternoon."

Aiming a quelling glance in his direction, Lucy said, "So I've been told. Perhaps after some groveling—"

"Perhaps *you* might grovel a bit, given what that young man has done for us," he countered, lowering a hip onto the arm of Maria's chair. He leaned over and kissed her forehead.

Her eyes rounding both at seeing his blatant display of affection as well as at hearing his words, Lucy held back her initial response.

She had hoped to take some revenge against Marcus Higgins. Hearing she might have to grovel instead had her thoughts all in a jumble.

When she glanced down at the baby, she was

stunned to discover him staring up at her, a grin on his face that brought with it a tiny dimple much like her brother's.

"Oh, all right," she whispered to her nephew. "You've convinced me."

CHAPTER 25
AN AFTERNOON CALLER ARRIVES

*L**ater that afternoon*

"Aren't you coming with me?" Jane, Dowager Viscountess Reardon, asked of her daughter. "We have morning calls to make and good news to share."

Lucy tittered. "Not today, Mother."

"You can't hold that baby all day. You'll spoil him," Jane warned. "And your arms will feel as if they're going to fall off when you finally do put him down."

Despite what everyone expected would be her reaction to learning she was the grandmother of an heir and therefore a dowager viscountess, Jane Burroughs Fitzsimmons had reacted in a most unexpected manner to meeting the boy in question.

She had greeted him with tear-filled eyes, introduced herself, and proceeded to hold him and talk to him for nearly an hour during breakfast.

"I won't. Besides, I'm expecting a caller," Lucy explained.

Her mother sniffed and took her leave.

Still in her arms, Antonio was wide awake but apparently unbothered it wasn't his mother who held him.

Lucy was about to go back to the salon when Peters answered a knock at the front door. She paused and watched as the butler greeted the caller.

She recognized his voice.

The odd manner in which her body responded—a pleasant flip in her middle had her inhaling softly—reminded her of the vivid dream she had experienced featuring Marcus.

She glanced down at the babe, surprised to discover he was smiling.

"He started doing that on the ship home," Marcus said. He stood directly in front of her, his hat held in one hand. "Of course he would do it for you. He's no fool," he added.

Lucy glanced up, swallowing when she saw how he gazed at her. "How do?" she managed, unprepared for seeing not a boy but a man standing before her. It was Marcus, but he appeared older, more mature since the kiss they had shared only ten days ago.

Ten days?

Perhaps it was because of the tanned face he displayed, no doubt from being aboard a ship and spending most of his time out of doors. Or mayhap it was because he had been eating at a captain's table. Or maybe it was because of what she had dreamt of doing with him in the middle of the night.

Her insides did that funny flip again, and she inhaled softly.

He lowered his lips to the hand that rested on the baby. "I am well," he replied, although his words suggested he wasn't. He was staring at the ring her brother had given her.

"You look well," she whispered. "Oh, it's just paste," she added, realizing why he seemed so sad. "My brother gave it to me so people would believe I was betrothed to you. So I wouldn't have to be a wallflower." When he didn't immediately reply, she asked, "What is it?"

Furrowing his brows, he seemed reluctant to respond. "I was told I should expect you to slap me," he said. His held his head up and to one side, as if he was giving her a clear target to hit.

"I was told to slap you," she replied. She rolled her eyes. "Maria might have mentioned I was supposed to. But I've decided I won't. I'm holding a baby, after all."

Marcus chuckled softly. "I appreciate that." He hesitated a moment before adding, "Lady Reardon said you would kiss me."

Lucy angled her head to one side. "I will, but my brother said I should grovel first."

Marcus furrowed a brow. "I think *I'm* the one who is supposed to grovel," he countered. "I'm so sorry for how it all happened," he said in a quiet voice. "When Frank told me about Lady Pettigrew's penchant for gossip, I felt awful," he explained. "I trusted her—"

"What's this?" Lucy asked, a brow rising in alarm.

Marcus displayed a look of dismay. "I wanted us to be discovered. So you would have to agree to marry me, because I've held you in such high regard for so long, and if I had returned from my Grand Tour and learned you had married someone else, I would... well, I don't know what I would have done," he blurted. "And then you proposed that wager, and I suddenly realized it was all going to work out. I was going to win either way."

Lucy scoffed. Torn between slapping him or arguing her case, she opted to argue. "How is it you think *you* won the wager?" she asked in disbelief. "We were discovered. *I* won the wager."

Marcus shrugged. "What if we amended that wager so that I not only marry you but also give you the ten thousand pounds?"

Scoffing again, Lucy dared a glance down at the babe she held, stunned at seeing his expression of delight. "You haven't got ten thousand pounds."

"Well, not on my person, but I shall in a few year's time," he replied. "After we return from our wedding trip to the Kingdom of the Two Sicilies," he added, holding his breath for a moment in anticipation of her response.

Lucy's eyes rounded. "You can afford that?" she asked in surprise.

He shrugged. "I was on my way, and I would have been gone for two years, but..." He indicated the baby. "It was more important to see to it he and his mother made it back to Lord Reardon," he said, grinning at seeing how the babe stared at him. "So... I figure the two of us can go for at least a year on the same funds," he reasoned.

She inhaled and let the breath out in a huff. "So... are we done then?" she asked, her eyes lighting up with mischief.

"What... what do you mean?" he stammered.

"Can we just get on with it?" She lifted the babe a few inches. "I want one of these."

Marcus glanced down and grinned when he saw how the baby seemed to be taking even more delight at hearing their exchange. "Well, I can definitely help with that," he stated. "But... first you have to marry me."

"I will when you propose," she countered, lifting her chin.

"I'll do you one better," he said, reaching into a waistcoat pocket. He held up a ring. "Miss Lucy Fitzsimmons, will you do me the honor of becoming my wife?"

Lucy stared at the ring. "I'll do *you* one better, Mr. Higgins."

"Oh?"

"Yes, I'll marry you, *and* I'll be the lady of Pendleton House."

Marcus lifted her hand from atop the babe, pulled the paste ring from her finger, and slid the larger, real sapphire version into place. "You have yourself a deal," he replied. "So... can we seal it with a kiss?" he asked, his manner tentative.

Lucy wiggled her fingers as she admired the ring and then reached up to place the same hand on the side of his face. "I thought you'd never ask."

He kissed her much like they had in the Weatherstone gardens, their lips at first barely touching and then locking into place. Then he deepened the kiss by touching her teeth with his tongue. When hers tangled with his, he moaned his appreciation. He might have continued kissing her all afternoon but for the cry of complaint that suddenly erupted between them.

They broke apart and stared down at the babe who would soon be his nephew. "After all I did for you?" Marcus said in dismay.

The babe grinned at the same moment a fart sounded.

CHAPTER 26
EPILOGUE

hree years later, Hyde Park

"This is the exact spot. I'm sure of it," Marcus announced, stopping to lower a picnic basket to the ground.

"I would have thought it was over there," Frank argued, pointing to another spot in the lawn of Hyde Park where they had played as children.

"I saw Lucy first *here*," Marcus insisted, pointing to the ground. "I fell in love with her right here."

"Well, I first saw Marianne over there," Frank stated.

Lucy and Marianne exchanged glances of amusement. "Then let's have our luncheon halfway in between," Lucy suggested. "Before your son starts eating the grass."

Marcus hurried over and scooped up the one-year-old. "Lucas, there will none of that," he said, lifting the boy into the air.

Lucas giggled in delight as his gown flew up to expose his pudgy legs.

Behind them, her brother and Maria had been strolling through the park at a more leisurely pace. Although three-year-old Antonio was fast on his feet and quite willing to run the entire distance to the picnic spot, the almost one-year-old whose hands were gripped between her parents was taking her first tentative steps. The poke bonnet Jane wore nearly hid her dark hair and large brown eyes.

"You must tell me all about your wedding trip," Lucy insisted, spreading out a blanket.

"Well, it certainly wasn't like yours," Marianne replied, unfurling a blanket a few feet away. Two years earlier, Lucy and Marcus had returned from Rome, Lucy already increasing with their first babe, Barbara. "But Frank arranged the most wonderful places for us to stay in the Peak District. Gorgeous views and plenty of entertainments. The food was even good," she gushed. "I hadn't known before I married him that his family had a country estate there."

"I always wondered how you could wait so long for Frank to return from his Grand Tour," Lucy said, grinning when Barbara opened the basket and began setting out the foods onto the blanket. Every time she bent over, the skirts of the pink gown she wore flipped up so her white petticoats and drawers were on display. "I think I would have gone mad."

"Oh, it wasn't so bad," Marianne countered. "He wrote often. Mostly complaints about Sinclair and

Hornsby since the two never learned enough Italian. They relied on him to translate on their behalf, which was probably a good thing since it meant they weren't about to abandon him somewhere along the way."

Lucy tittered. "As I recall, you were keeping your betrothal secret from your mother. How long did that last?"

Marianne giggled, her gaze going to where Frank and Marcus were tossing a rubber ball with the other children. "More than a year. Father was the one who let it slip during dinner one night. You should have seen Mother's face."

"Oh, dear. Was she angry with him?"

"Vexed, of course," Marianne said, exaggerating her raised brows by waggling them. "Which is exactly why he said something about Frank becoming his son. I don't think I ever saw my mother so surprised."

"So she never noticed your ring?"

Marianne shook her head. "Oh, she thought Father had given it to me for my birthday," she said. "I should have corrected her, but I didn't want to disappoint Father since it was his plan all along to vex her."

Lucy shook her head. "I should hope Marcus and I never wish to deliberately vex one another," she said, waving for Maria and Christopher to join them.

The two spread out their own blanket, and Christopher immediately laid down, angling his top hat to shield his eyes from the sun. Meanwhile, Maria saw to unloading the contents of their basket onto the blanket.

Their oldest had already joined his cousin to play

with the ball, but Jane toddled over to where Barbara had settled on the blanket with her doll. She collapsed onto her bottom, sending the two into a fit of giggles.

"As I recall, that wager vexed you quite a bit," Marianne remarked.

"It was my wager," Lucy reminded her. "One we both claimed to have won." She grinned at the memory of it.

"Well, you did marry," Marianne said, "But did you ever get the ten thousand pounds?"

Lucy grinned in delight. "Why do you think it is we're out here celebrating today?" she asked, pulling Jane into her arms so she could give her niece a hug.

Marianne's eyes widened. "He gave you ten thousand pounds?" she asked in surprise.

"Had it put into an account with my name on it only yesterday. Then I promptly asked him to reinvest half of it on my behalf."

Marcus joined them to help himself to a sandwich. "So, Mrs. Turnbridge, has my wife told you she's rich?" he asked before giving Lucy a peck on her cheek.

"Marcus," Lucy gently scolded. "Don't be cheeky."

"Just this very moment," Marianne claimed. "Now could you please explain to Frank how you did it so I might be rich, too?"

"Already did," Marcus replied.

"He told me, too," Christopher called out, his face still half hidden by his hat.

Marcus ignored his brother-in-law, but his eyes rounded. "Oh, so Frank hasn't told you?" he said to Marianne. His attention went to where his best friend was pushing a large stick into the ground, apparently marking the spot where he had first laid eyes on the girl who would become his wife fifteen years later.

Marianne's eyes widened. "No," she breathed in disbelief. She glanced over at Frank, who was summoning her with a crooked finger. "But I think I'm about to learn of it." She struggled to her feet and shook out her skirts.

"Pretend you're surprised," Marcus whispered.

"I don't think she needs to pretend, darling," Lucy whispered, grinning as she watched her friend run to her husband.

Christopher chuckled and sat up, pulling Maria into his arms. His startled wife gave a yelp. "About time *we* went for a wedding trip, don't you suppose?" he asked.

"And here I'd thought you'd forgotten," she replied, settling herself against the front of his body.

"Shall we go to Spain?"

She furrowed her dark brows and turned her head to regard him with a look of annoyance. "I want to go to Rome," she replied. "To all the places they went," she added, waving a hand to indicate Marcus and Lucy.

"With the children?" he asked in surprise.

Marcus and Lucy exchanged quick glances. "We'll see to them while you're gone," Marcus offered.

"We will, and they have their nurse," Lucy added.

"So... I should arrange passage on a ship," Christopher remarked.

"You should go on *The Fairweather*," Marcus

suggested. "Prove to Captain St. John you really are alive."

"Oh, I already did that," Christopher said.

"You didn't punch him in the nose, did you?" Lucy asked, worried her brother might have used violence against the man who had accidentally kept him from his wife.

"No," Christopher assured them. "I took him for a pint of ale or two." When he didn't offer anything else, Maria once again turned to regard him with a questioning look. "And?" she prompted.

"And I... I reimbursed him for your passage from Valencia."

"And?" Lucy asked, apparently already aware of what else he had done to the hapless captain.

"Oh," he grunted, glancing in the direction of Frank and Marianne to see the two in an embrace. "I might have made a wager with him that I won," he finally admitted.

"What did you win?" Maria asked with excitement.

Christopher chuckled, his amusement sounding almost diabolical. "I got to push him into the Thames."

Marcus gasped. "Remind me never to make a wager with *you*," he said, grinning.

CHAPTER 27
AUTHOR NOTES

The Grand Tour

Throughout Europe and England, the Grand Tour afforded young men the ability to complete their formal Classics education by traveling to the locations they had studied in university. The trips allowed them to experience culture, view fine art, and tour Ancient Greek and Roman sites, and the itineraries most often included at least what is now Italy and sometimes Greece and other European countries.

The expression 'Grand Tour' itself originated with Richard Lassels, a 17th century Roman Catholic priest and travel writer who used it in his guidebook *The Voyage of Italy*. Published in 1670, the book suggested touring with a tutor by first crossing the Channel, traveling in a coach through France (which didn't happen during England's wars with France, of course), and from there, venturing onto Italy and sometimes Sicily and Greece. The average Grand Tour lasted one year, although the sons of wealthier British aristocrats were gone as long as two years or more.

The tours weren't always educationally oriented, however. For some, the promise of independence was more important. Venice was popular with pleasure seekers since it offered occasions for drinking, partying, and gambling.

Despite the French Revolution's adverse effect on most Grand Tour plans, the practice of going on one continued for young aristocrats well into the nineteenth century.

*Z*any
Much as it does today, the term zany was used during the Regency era to describe those who were eccentric or absurd, goofy or clownish. Had he been a little less so, Viscount Thistlewaite could have been called a 'blade.'

ABOUT THE AUTHOR

A self-described nerd and lover of science, Linda Rae spent many years as a published technical writer specializing in 3D graphics workstations, software and 3D animation (her movie credits include SHREK and SHREK 2). Mythology, immortality, and ancient Greece have been lifelong interests.

A fan of action-adventure movies, she can frequently be found at the local cinema. Although she no longer has any tropical fish, she does follow the San Jose Sharks. She makes her home in Cody, Wyoming.

For more information:
www.lindaraesande.com
Sign up for Linda Rae's newsletter:
Regency Romance with a Twist

9 781946 271761